[signature]

May you always fight

A RINGLANDER NOVELLA

———

THE BATTLE THAT WAS LOST

———

MICHAEL S. JACKSON

@mikestepjack | mjackson.co.uk

CONTENTS

ACKNOWLEDGMENTS

Since I began this journey, I've been adopted by an incredible community of independent published writers who produce just the best stories out there.

Some of those people helped me write this novella, as beta readers and editors. Their excellent feedback not only helped shape this story, but also the Ringlander world and series too. Thank you all so much: Jennifer Coltherd, T. L. Greylock, Peter Hutchinson, Megan Moss, Madeleine Svensson & Thomas Turner.

To my dearest friend, Liam. I included you in this story as a soldier because that's how I will always see you. Despite the odds, you faced life with a grim determination, to win and to learn, to protect and to nurture. To me these are the traits of a fighter and a soldier, and I feel privileged to have stood in line with you.

May you always fight.

THE WORLD OF

RENGAS

Nortun

Laich

Makril

Way mouth

FAIRSKY

Vasen

Teräyä

TYR

The Way

KRASK

E

May you always fight

THE BATTLE THAT WAS LOST

DALI (SOMEWHERE NORTH OF DRAKEMYRE)

Staegrim shook his head at the heaps of dead horses barely a hundred paces south.

"It's a strange thing."

The Bohr were inhuman, a cross between a man and bull standing, and twice as tall. There were eight or nine of them within the folds of fighting soldiers standing like great stalks of wheat amongst the grass. Still, it wasn't the Bohr that had done this. This mess of dead animals was an altogether human endeavour, and worse, it was the side Staegrim found himself fighting for.

"A strange thing indeed."

His partner Qor ran her hand through her greasy hair. "Shut up, Stae."

"I mean, I would have, at the very least, eaten them before just sending them to their deaths like they don't mean anything," said Staegrim, trying to find the positives of losing an entire regiment of war animals. "And all so the rebels can win a handful of pine trees in the middle of the battlefield."

"Stae..."

"And they're in the bloody way! How are we to get up the

hill now? We'll have to climb over the damned things before we even get close to the Bohr command. Let alone come close to assassinating anyone!"

"Stae! Fucking shut it."

Staegrim chuckled, and Qor rolled her eyes. It wasn't the gallows humour that made him laugh, as most thought. It was anxiety. He got all tight-chested sometimes, though he couldn't say why. It was just the way he was put together. The panic would build like a cup overflowing, and usually for no reason. It was there now, lurking, threatening to overtake his senses. He focused on the real things of this world, the trees, the soldiers dying downhill, the four of them here skulking in the bushes like frightened rabbits—anything outside of his own head. He glanced at the two men behind Qor, but they were silent as his mammy's grave. Perhaps the reality of their predicament was dawning upon them.

He nodded to the big one. "Wouldn't you say, eh, Kav? Imagine killing twenty good beasts just to gain a foothold in a fight. It's a bloody waste is what it is. Wouldn't you say, Kav? Kav?"

The Keeper of Horses looked the product of a Bohr himself, all muscles and hair. He was so big he made the few needlepines around them look small. The man grimaced in Staegrim's direction, apparently holding back some sort of emotion. "It just...I can't even...Why kill them?" he uttered.

"Stop your belly aching, Kav," said Qor. "Look, there's still one or two alive and kicking down there. Bet you could still ride one if you could catch the arsing thing, although, it's probably a bit muddy for that. I doubt even a good rider could gallop through that bog." The yellows of Qor's eyes flashed again. "We're barely a league from Drakemyre and the most famous markets in the Ringland. You can pick up some more when all this fighting is said and done. They're just fucking animals, Kavik."

Kavik rounded on her. "*Just* animals? They're mine. They keep me as I keep them. Do you have no faith about you at all, girl?"

Qor squared her shoulders. If she were a cat, her hips would be wiggling, readying a pounce. Kavik, Forbringr bless him, stood there as oblivious as an idiot bear.

"Faith is for the fallen," hissed Qor, adjusting her leather armour.

Anyone else (in their right mind) would have quailed under Kavik's glare, even Staegrim, and he had seen things. Granted, he had never seen a horse charge used as bait before. Whoever had designed this little skirmish hated animals, that much was as clear as...well, it was pretty fucking clear. Still, Staegrim wasn't one to question the high-ups—he was a bastard—that's why he was here.

Duga's eyes narrowed. No one else saw it, but Staegrim did. Duga was one of them high-ups, and the orders came from him. If ever a shadow could be said to take on flesh, it was this man, this rebel officer.

"It's not for us to question Laeb's orders," rasped Duga, his voice a blade. "Commander Suilven orders his officers, his officers order Tactician Laeb. Laeb turns those orders, those goals, into results. This is the third engagement we've had with the Bohr and the third we'll win. Above all though, Laeb is a captain. To disrespect him is to disrespect the Tsiorc."

"And the Tsiorc are..."

Qor punched Staegrim in the back. "The rebels you fuck-wit. The side we're on."

"Alright! It's just a strange name is all. What's it even mean?"

Duga drew a long breath. "I didn't recruit you in the hope you would question all that I say. Just that you would *do* all I say."

"We ain't no recruits."

"Stae..."

"Well, we're not. We're bastards. Bastards get paid. Recruits get stomped on. There's a big difference."

Kavik stepped forward, and Staegrim flinched. "You'll do as we tell you or you'll get not a penny, chit or mark."

"A chit is the same as a penny, if you were from Rengas you might know that." Staegrim held out his hands—this was getting ridiculous. "Look. Alls I'm saying is that it's a strange thing to do, so it is. Sending all those horses into the grinder like that. Course they were going to be killed. It's a waste. And like you said, Kav, now you're left standing here with the three of us, hidden amongst the bushes watching as your pets—"

"Pets?"

Staegrim silently chastised himself. He'd been on a roll, and it was something even his good mammy, Forbringr rest her soul, told him not to do. He just wasn't clever enough. Qor frowned at him. She would have found the right words, he was sure.

Kavik's glare hardened. "They're my brethren, bastard."

"Careful," growled Qor. "Bastard or no. He has a name."

"And what is a bastard, girl?"

"A fool who cleans up after bigger fools!"

Kavik flung out his arm to gesture at the open expanse of land beyond the needlepines. "Then leave! I'm sure the commander wouldn't want anyone here who don't want to be here! Go. Leave us be!"

Qor's gaze followed Kavik's outstretched hand. "Alls I said was to mind your words, horse master. Don't be talking down to us or we'll take our business elsewhere. By the looks of things so far, you rebels look like you need all the help you can get."

"Right," said Staegrim, tapping Qor's shoulder. "Now that we've finished wasting everyone's time. What's the plan?"

"The plan?" Duga stood up in the thicket, his dappled coat and breeches blending perfectly with the fauna. "The plan is we press on. The horses did their job, and they did it well. The lords believe they just finished off our surprise cavalry flanks." He turned to Kavik. "The cost for this ground was high, Kavik, but it will be worth it. Laeb had no choice, given how quickly the engagement began." He nodded down the rise towards the black-armoured lines of the lords' army, moving assuredly forward into the rebel's half of the valley. "No one in their right mind would have believed we'd willingly sacrifice so many just so four men could make it unseen to a copse of trees in the middle of the battleground. Yet here we are standing between the enemy leaders and their own army."

"Aye," said Qor, "and what can two bastards and two cunts do against an entire army?"

Duga's stare hardened. Qor knew exactly why they were here, but she did so like to antagonise people. It was one of the things Staegrim loved about her even if Duga didn't take the bait this time.

"Now, now," said Staegrim. "Let's keep things civil."

"If you're not up to the task—"

"Oh, I wouldn't say that." Qor's cut-throat was suddenly in her hand, rolling her over her fingers, her stance all sideways, ready for fighting. She unfolded the blade.

"Put it away," ordered Staegrim. "Now." Blessedly, the girl did as she was told. "Duga, we're just looking out for ourselves is all. The world is a savage place, and this is murderous work. We're used to dark deeds down dark alleys, but here we stand on the field of battle where life is at its cheapest."

Duga's glare softened a hair. "Then let us get on with it. So you may return to those dark deeds." He turned and beckoned Kavik away from them.

Qor offered Staegrim a glance then stooped low and picked her way between the trunks mumbling more about wasting time. Staegrim stood, feeling dumb, waiting for something more, but all had been said. He turned to follow her and caught some of Duga and Kavik's conversation.

"Kavik, not a word of the bastards to Laeb."

"I won't keep secrets from the man, Duga. He wouldn't keep secrets from us. We owe him that and more besides."

Duga seemed to hesitate, and even as Staegrim skulked slowly forward after Qor, he knew Duga had replaced his cowl.

"Secrets keep only their keepers. I'm ordering you not to tell Laeb about the bastards. Understand?"

Kavik didn't respond, but Staegrim got the impression the man had taken the order. The grey grass within the copse crunched underfoot as Staegrim took his place behind Qor. Staegrim the Feared was what those in Drakemyre called him. He could be silent. He could be deadly (if the coin was right). Yet there was more than coin at work here. And something told him to keep his wits close by.

THE SHADOW IN THE SMALL VALLEY HAD NOTHING TO DO with the rolling clouds painting patterns upon the hills, nor the incessant rain making fools of the men and women fighting below.

The shadow was the oncoming slaughter. The unstoppable. The inevitable. A desperate animal hungry for the taste of flesh, and it was here for Laeb. It was here for the Tsiorc.

It was a strange feeling to know you would not live to meet the new day, though one he had been sure his future self would have been prepared for. Yet here he was, and his mind was no different. His future self was him and the curse of this forsaken Ringland was coming for him and him alone.

Captain Laeb surveyed the lines of soldiers below as he imagined many others had before him, generals and tacticians alike. But where they were confident, he was woeful. The so-called lord's army was comprised of Kemen mercenaries paid in gold and ordered to fight by the massive Bohr leading each regiment. Five Tsiorc regiments versus eight of the lords, tightly-packed and well-trained. The Tsiorc were following his standard butterfly pattern as much as they could, but the lines were thinly spread, and the wings of the formation were being held back by the high hills. The lords were focusing their strength on a drill down through the centre using a modified flying duck tactic—crude but effective.

Laeb checked the strapping on his leather armour and heeled his animal forward.

"Captain, wait! You can't be serious."

Laeb turned to commander Suilven. "In Sulitar, the tacticians work from the battlefield, not from above it. I'd wager the only thing missing from your side is a tea cart so you may watch the death of your fellows in even greater comfort." Before Suilven could respond, he added, "Are you afraid to get your hands dirty, Commander? Up here on your hill?"

It was a dangerous tactic to be so blithe with the Tsiorc leader, a greying rock of a man with the strength of two besides, but Laeb had a responsibility to push and drive these soldiers forward—it was their survival at stake here, not victory nor accolade. What had begun as a surprise skirmish became a chaotic tangle of unruly lines. If this battle was a game of Chinaes, then it had started strong but quickly descended into chaos, which would leave them with nothing but high losses on both sides. Losses the Tsiorc couldn't afford.

Both armies slid on the liquid ground, which barely two

hours previous had been baked solid. Dali was like that, one moment cold enough to make Nord seem like a place to grow old, the next there was no escape from the harsh sunlight but to dig a hole in the hard earth. The same could be said about its people, hard and changeable—Daliaens were still some of the best fighters out there, not as good as Sulitarians, mind you, but good for a Ringland force.

"No," said Suilven, riding over to Laeb. "The answer is simple. We just need to apply more pressure forwards."

"That I agree with, Commander. We need to slow that V-shape of the lords' front lines or they will cut through us like a smith's chisel through slag. Then the Bohr and their lord's army will roll over me, you, and your tea cart."

Laeb raised his hand and a young flagbearer rushed over.

"Yes, Captain?" His salute was as misshapen as the fuzz open his chin.

"Order the fourth to retreat and the fifth to reorganise and push forward."

"Belay that!" growled Suilven. "You can't push the regiment in! They'll all be killed."

"A sacrifice here, gives leverage there." Laeb pointed to the diagonal lines of the Bohr army pressing against the regiments of Tsiorc. "If we can penetrate the—"

"I said no," said the commander. "You mean to create a gap, only to fill it with new fighters? The enemy will pour in like water into a hole. We are not sacrificing so many for such little gain."

"The chances—"

"Are too slim. We need something else."

Laeb quelled the frustration building in his stomach. Barely two hundred paces downhill, the Tsiorc were fighting for their lives. Even up here, the Bohr's animal faces were visible, snarling and snapping at the Tsiorc soldiers, while their muscled torsos, covered in thick leathery skin, tore through the rebel lines with disturbing ease. They had yet to fell one of these beasts, and the fight around them created knots in the lines. With every knot that formed, the surrounding lines grew weaker. The lords were winning.

Laeb tried to quiet his mind—to focus on the goal—but his head was full to bursting with clever movements and ideas: draw the flanking sides inward, set the pitch alight on the right flank, force the enemy to run into larger pools on the left flank, send in the explosive cartridges… "Perhaps the answer is to squeeze the flanks and create a bottleneck."

Commander Suilven blinked at him. "And cut off this duck's head. The mottled nara he sat upon shook its head against the rain, but gently. Kavik trained his animals well—those sharp antlers were feared by a prudent enemy. If they got out of this, Laeb owed the horsekeeper a large drink. Perhaps a whole tavern.

After a long moment the commander shook his head. "Too risky."

"Then I should get down there."

"To lead?"

"To fight."

"Captain. We cannot afford to let you fight. It sets an awkward precedent." The officers behind him shook their heads in the same way, muttering amongst themselves like schoolchildren. Suilven nodded towards the adjacent hillside across the valley where the tents of the enemy general stood tall. "They're not even watching. Are they so sure of victory, so practiced in their expectations that they will not even command their armies?"

"Say what you like about mercenaries, commander. They know how to fight." Laeb shook his head. "The general will come out soon. Then the reason for the loss of so many animals will be very clear."

Suilven didn't look convinced. "I hope you're right. I put

my life on the line by taking you in, tactician. Yet we find ourselves staring death in the face once more. I find that I know the fellow so well, I could recite his name. We just...we need more resource. We are outnumbered three to one."

"The wings of our butterfly are strong. Our flanks will hold. The unhappy truth is that we will have to accept some losses before we see some returns. And if you don't want to sacrifice any—"

"No, I do not."

"Then strengthening the back lines will buy us time."

"Strengthen them with who?" snapped Suilven. "We have no one left! The Bohr will break through, and then all that stands between them and the top of this hill is us!" Suilven's expression grew hard. "Order the retreat."

Laeb shut his eyes. "Then it is the end." Sadness swept over him. "The end of the Tsiorc."

A CLAP OF THUNDER TORE THROUGH THE AIR, AND THE battlefield held its breath. The echo of the storm above permeated the ground beneath Staegrim's feet. It was a strange thing to consider that even the very earth could be so affected by sound. Or was it those fighting upon it? Two sides, battling each other for whatever advantage they could gain. Perhaps the thunder was the Forbringr, the great Gods of the earth, the rocks, and the hills, coming alive to aid the rebel Tsiorc. He doubted highly they would survive this day on their own.

"Stae, the ground is rumbling."

"I feel it, Qor. That's what happens when five thousand pairs of feet stomp around each other in unison."

"Like a dance," grinned Qor. "As long it is that and not some other shit we are yet to see."

"Well, they say—"

"The east regiments are flagging," uttered Duga, his mottled face hidden in the gloom. The waver in his voice was harder for the shadow to conceal.

Staegrim cast his gaze east. The regiments were there, steel cutting through raindrops and flesh alike.

"There is no use in our joining, Duga," said Kavik. "It will only get us killed that little bit faster. Before we've had a chance to complete our mission. The tide may yet be turned."

Duga shook his head slowly. "Some tides are inevitable, Horse Master. They may never be stopped."

Staegrim followed Duga's stare back to where the Tsiorc officers stood safe upon the ridgetop, then let his gaze sweep over the battlefield to the tents on the opposite side. The Bohr enemy leaders were absent, apparently happy to let their army fight without direction. Was that foolhardiness or confidence. In Staegrim's experience the two amounted to the same thing.

The Kemen Empire stood south of the border lands below the Way channel and stretched for three thousand leagues all the way to the other end of the Middle Sea. The humans who carved a life for themselves in such harsh and hot lands probably found Nord a welcome break and the Ringleaders as soft as a babe's pillow. There was no greater force within the upper circle of the world, nothing that straddled Nord, nor Dali nor even the mythical land of Sulitar where fighters were said to be harder than stone and grown from the very earth, came close to the lord's army. The well-fought and well-paid Kemen mercenaries were a black tide that would wash away the rebels.

"I'm here for the coin, blue-eyes, but don't think that means we'll be throwing our lives away for you now."

"Then why do you hesitate?" hissed Duga, too quietly for anyone else to hear. "Because you know, that coin or not, the lives of all humans depend on the rebels. You know it. I can smell it all over you."

"Stae's got a point there," said Qor. "We ain't here to—Wait!" She stopped, gaze fixed on the new flag being raised on the hill. "They're retreating! The Tsiorc are retreating!"

"And there's our signal!" said Duga. "Laeb said a retreat might come and damn the man if he doesn't have the eyes of the gods for seeing it first." He pulled some silver tube cartridges from inside his coat. "Three bombs, Kavik. Aim for the Bohr fighters."

Kavik nodded. "I've a strong arm."

"And you're faster than any of us on the animals." Duga pointed to the dead animals, among which a few live ones were idly wandering, having escaped the slaughter. He pointed to the top of one of the cylinders. "Bang the top as hard as you can, then throw. That sparks the fuse. And mind, they'll go off at even the slightest bump, so ride smooth." He brought his fist to his chest. "May you always fight."

Kavik nodded, scooped the silver tubes into the crook of one arm, and took off down the hill at a speed that defied all logic. He leapt upon the back of a young horse and galloped off down the valley towards the rear of the lord's army. Stopping in the centre he lobbed three spots of light deep into the lines of soldiers. A long second later, Staegrim saw three bursts of fire, each followed by a clap of thunder, that hurt his ears, then man, woman, and Bohr alike were thrown forty paces into the air, while the rest were felled like stalks of wheat in a blizzard.

Qor clapped like a child watching festival lights. "Woo! That should even up the fight a bit!"

"By the Forbringr's arsehole!" Staegrim turned to Duga. "Why would you keep those in your pocket? Are you mad?"

But Duga wasn't watching. His gaze was on the tents on

the opposite ridge, now emptying out as the Bohr officers came out to watch the carnage unfolding in the valley.

"Is that him?" said Staegrim.

Duga nodded slowly. "That's him." A wicked smile grew across his face. "Our target."

THE FOUR TSIORC GUARDS SPRANG FORWARDS FROM THE command post upon the Tsiorc's hill, running towards the group of lords that had broken through the rebel lines. Laeb hefted his curved bluesteel sword in his hand, unsure whether to stay mounted or to get down and fight.

"Your place is here!" growled Suilven.

The guards were skilled but outnumbered. The lead guard flicked his narrow pinblade, dragging it over tendon and muscle alike, but with each dead mercenary, two more took their place.

"Close the lines!" roared Laeb. "Close the damn lines! Don't let them through!"

"Commander—"

A bright spot of fire bloomed from towards the back of lords' lines, the soldiers already flying through the air before the sound caught up with the action.

"Finally," said Laeb.

Two more explosions came in quick succession; their pointed attack reduced to a scant outline of bewildered and deafened men stumbling between three craters.

"Close the lines! Now! Now is the time!" Laeb heeled his nara forward, and the beast leapt eagerly down the hill. Steel flashed by him on the right as the lead guard's last victim fell. Slowing just enough, Laeb reached down and hauled the Tsiorc guard up on the nara's back, and they rushed towards the broken rebel lines.

"Captain!" shouted the lead guard, his plait bouncing behind in the wind. "Take us in!"

Laeb skillfully wove his animal between the pitched fighting, the chorus of steel on steel growing louder with each stride, and the lead guard roaring orders from behind him. "Reform the line! Front regiments, drive forward!"

The butterfly's body had to regain the ground lost by Duga's explosive cartridges, or it would soon be filled with the enemy again. They needed someone to drive them forward, or these strong wings—their spread flanks—would simply not be strong enough to hold back the more numerous lords.

" We can outmatch the skill of the lord veterans, Captain," said the lead guard. "but only while we are on equal ground."

"How many guards have you left?"

"Three, Captain."

"Split the broken lines into thirds and assign one of the guards to each, then follow me in."

The butterfly's wings could spread out, squeezing the three-ton legion of enemy soldiers into a bottleneck that would not so easily be cracked, but time, time was of the absolute essence. They had to push forward now, or it would all be over. This was the endgame.

"May you always fight!" The lead guard jumped off the nara's back and began herding some of the fresher Tsiorc soldiers in behind Laeb's nara, until soon there was a steady influx of fresh fighters heading towards the craters. The new blood began filling the gaps left by Duga's bombs and chopping at the still disoriented soldiers with great effect. Laeb glanced back at the hilltop to see the Tsiorc officer Magister Firam lifting the Tsiorc's tritone horn to his lips, and the sound of it echoed around the valley. The back rows of the lords' army down the hill marched into the space left by the ruined flying duck formation, strengthening the body. And the Tsiorc wings began to spread out wider and wider, gaining ground, then drawing back in, enclosing the enemy on all sides, tightening the noose. The battle was not yet lost.

There was no honour in it, some would say, but Staegrim certainly never thought of stealing that way. He was helping those in need. It just so happened that he was often the one who happened to be in need.

The whites of the seer's eyes flicked like he was falling into a day-sleep, nodding to questions unasked. "Yes. Yes, I see..." He held Stae-grim's palm higher, looking for something new and insightful, no doubt. His chains and crystal jewellery glittered like a starry night under the candles above, swaying as he moaned, cursed, and mumbled. He could ham it up all he wanted, and the longer he did, the longer Staegrim could worth him out.

Some people had the ability to cloak how they felt about things, but not Staegrim. He wore his heart on his sleeve, at least that was what his good mammy would say, but seers were notoriously slippery, saying one thing and meaning another entirely. As tempting as it was to learn about what might yet come in his life, a seer could only be trusted to the value of the coins in his hand. Everyone knew that.

The seer's eyes shifted again, just enough to keep an eye on him. Staegrim the Feared was a bastard, after all. Most could read it on him, like a board he wore on the streets. A board? That might get him some more work.

"Not a bad idea at all."

The seer opened his eyes. "You feel it too then?"

"Oh. Yes. I feel it. Feel it like it's right here in the room tickling my back." Staegrim bit his lip. He had no idea what he was saying. It seemed to work though, and the seer returned to his trance.

The smoky room was as you might expect, wall hangings, knick-

*knacks, cheap crystal, jars of beach stones, and not a coin in sight.
How, by the blood of the Forbringr, does a seer not have stacks of coins
just sitting about? The fake gold around his neck wouldn't get Staegrim barely a loaf of bread, let alone that suited, double breasted
jacket from Morlak's. Old Morlak himself was dead now of course—
his sons took over the boutique not long after, but his clothes were the
finest in all of Dali. Seaspun, silver-lined, ivory buttons, and the
finest lambswool. He shook his head. There was no way the shit
around this seer's neck would get him that jacket, not if he had a
barrelful of the shining stuff in the back. Staegrim needed to think
bigger.*

He stood up from the table. "Thank you, seer! I feel so replenished
and... free of mind." *He bumped into the chair as he backed out.* "It's a
wonderful place you have here. Wonderful. The colours, the smells.
You know your trade!"

"Do you not want to hear your future?"

Staegrim shook his head slowly. "Staegrim the Feared lives each
day as it comes. The Feared doesn't need—"

"The Feared?" *The man closed his eyes.* "Your mother gave you
that name. But not at birth. At death."

Staegrim frowned. The sounds of the busy street pulled at him.
"How did you know that?"

The seer smiled. "She told me."

"And do the dead talk often to you?"

"Sometimes. Not big things, but enough to get the measure of a
man. Occasionally the streams of reality cross, and in those moments,
those as I can see, reflections of things, some of which come to be,
others which do not. But all are decisions a man could make, a man
like you, Feared. The consequences of those choices are as clear to me as
the sky is to the bird."

"All right. I'm listening."

The seer shook his head. "What's it worth to you?"

"If you're really that attuned to the spirits of old, you would know
you talk to a man with no more than two bits to his name."

His eyes rolled back in his head. "Yes, she told me that too."

"You're a fucking lunatic."

"It has been said." The seer took Staegrim's hand. "So then, take what I offer for free. A named man has worth, and I see that your name will have worth, Feared. Treat it so, and the value of this name will carry you forward until one day it will be worth more than the breaths you take."

"You mean..."

"Yes. One day, your name will save your life, but only if you abide by the rules of your trade. The rules of the bastard."

The words swam from the seer's inked lips, dry and cracked and bloodied, and when he twisted the ring on Staegrim's finger and pulled it off, Staegrim the Feared just let him. It should have enraged him, and deep down in the pit of him, a fire consumed his resolve, the two battling for control. The meaning of the seer's words was too important to ignore. The word's themselves floated before him as abstract things, their significance a weight as heavy as lead impressing upon his mind. In the end though, it all took too long, and by the time Staegrim had anything resembling a handle of himself, the seer had gone. The heavy chenille curtains swayed, as though someone had just walked through them. Staegrim stood, confused but calm. Assured. Things would be all right. They always were for a bastard.

He breathed deep through his nostrils as his eyes adjusted to the light of the city. "Ah, the Drake!" Surely nothing could beat the bustling metropolis that was the city of Drakemyre. A capital of capitals! The sweeping lines of the hills gave the roads an almost sickly appearance to the newcomer, but he was getting used to them. Even in his short time here, he'd walked each of Drakemyre's roads and alleys twice over. He knew this city as well as the curves of his own hand. Maybe not as well as his home in Ston'rer or perhaps even Port Ataska, but Dali was a bigger country compared to the island of Anqamor. Or maybe it wasn't come to think of it. It didn't matter now in any case, he couldn't go back to Anqamor, even if he wanted to.

He stepped up onto a passing torqa, nodding as the driver turned to look at him.

"Two bits."

"Two?"

"Qeuatira dozemi," said the woman in accented Daliaen.

"Fine, but I want out right up at the Halven Estates." Stae grumbled as the torqa driver set off. A half mile for two bits in this town? This city used to be great. The wheels bounced over the cobbles until the tall viaducts began peaking over the tops of the greystone buildings. It was narrow here where the land got higher, but for some reason the scraps of the lower markets never made it up this high. Too common. To be fair, though, Staegrim the Feared was probably the most common scrap within two blocks anyway.

The tall archways loomed above as waves of stone, holding back the morning drizzle and leaving patches of dryness beneath. Staegrim wondered silently what condition the driver's feet must be in, running this little cart all over town, but that was her lot in life, carting people from here to there. You choose your own luck.

The narrow street opened out into a junction and the cart slowed.

"No, no. Further in. In!"

The cart driver stopped and turned on the spot between the long wooden cart handles. "No pay. No go."

Staegrim took another long breath. He'd been hoping to get out of this one, perhaps leaving the woman in an alleyway nursing a broken nose, a nose that looked like it had been broken many times before. Staegrim reached in and plucked two coins from his pocket: a Tyrian penny that was no longer in circulation and one bit.

The driver gave them a quick look, and still riding high from her win, they were off again up the hill to where the larger markets convened. The Halven Estates. It was here he would make his money back, a one-bit, one-penny ride for a hundred bits. Maybe even a silver mark or perhaps Daliaen gold. Oh, but it was good to be alive.

. . .

STAEGRIM SHOVED HIS BLADE IN THROUGH THE SOLDIER'S face with a satisfying crunch. Two hundred and forty-seven—that's how many people had died by his hand. He yanked the blade out, spraying blood and brains all over the place, and put the boot in her, sending her flying back into the rest of them like bowling pins. He wasn't fond of killing much, but if the job asked for it. Well. It was always good to enjoy your work.

"Qor?"

"What?!"

"You remember when we first met?"

Qor flicked her blade up in the air and the enemy soldier in front watched it like a moth to a flame. He didn't see Qor take a step back, nor did he see the haymaker she planted into his jaw. The jawbreaker. A fucking classic! As the man reeled, she caught the blade as it fell, and stabbed him in the guts with the pointed end. "Of course," she said, breathless. "Why?" She kicked the man off and he slid to the mud.

"I was just thinking about—shit! Watch your right!"

And she was off again. Battles were hardly the place to stand around reminiscing.

"Should we not be sneaking up to the Bohr camp?" shouted Staegrim, turning to Duga. "Why are we fighting here? Where are the other squads?"

Duga parried, stepped back, and thrust forward, killing a man as efficiently as if he were pulling on trousers. He paused just long enough to glance sidelong at Staegrim, then bounded forward for the next lord soldier, repeating the process. Parry, back, and thrust, parry, back, and thrust. "Are you asking me... if we should be here... in the midst of things, fighting to stay alive?" he growled, throwing in an extra surge of effort to cut the legs out from under one unfortunate soldier.

Staegrim frowned. "I guess so."

"Then... it would seem..." Duga unceremoniously pushed his blade in through a soldier's neck. "I would have to say... no."

Staegrim leant back as a sword poked in at him—one of Qor's cast offs. But she made it right and pulled the man back and opened his throat with her knife. Qor was a natural born killer, which was hilarious considering her upbringing.

"Watch what you're bloody doing! That one almost got me."

"Don't want to get blood on your shiny leather armour, then don't join the battle. Now, are you gonna let me finish the last of this lot off or not?"

She leapt into the last three like a tigress, slashing and biting and killing.

"Forbringr's blood!" Duga stood barely a hair's breadth from him. Staegrim wanted to recoil, but something told him to stand his ground. "You scared the shit outa—"

"When I met you in Drakemyre," hissed Duga, "did I ask for your life story?"

"You did not," said Staegrim, thumbing his nose and trying to appear unfazed.

"What *did* I ask you?"

"You wanted to know how much coin a bastard would want." Staegrim knew this was a trap, but damn it if he wasn't clever enough to see where it was leading. "You know, to kill the Kael."

Duga's eyes widened, and he thrust his sword forward, right underneath Staegrim's arm through his leather strapping, and into the lord who had snuck up behind them. Duga shouldered him out of the way cutting the lord down like a sapling, a sapling holding a mace the size of a watermelon.

"You know..." Duga yanked his sword out of the man's ribcage. "In Sulitar, money has little meaning. It doesn't define our lives like it does here. Honour is our currency." He pointed at the corpse of the lord. "This fellow would have caved your head in had I not been here. I just saved your life. If I had not, then the ten coins I gave you in Drakemyre would have only served to make your corpse's pockets heavier before lining the pockets of whoever happened to bury you. Your partner, at a guess."

"I've killed less than I've been saved, so what's your point."

Duga closed his eyes and took a deep breath. "This is the Tsiorc's last stand. We came here not to fight, but to die. There was no expectation that we would walk away from this battle. There are no other squads or forces. This is us. The last of the Bohr resistance. The last rebels. Barely two thousand men and the hill we came to die on." He stepped closer. "So, know that when I say these words, I absolutely mean them, bastard. Your life is worth not a tenth of mine, nor a hundredth of a Tsiorc solider. Your life is worth no more to me than the ten pieces of metal I dropped into your hand. Same goes for her."

"Her name is Qor."

"I. Don't. Care." He stepped closer with every syllable. "You are here to do a job. You are here because I paid you to be here." He tossed a coin and Staegrim snatched it out of the air.

"Why—"

"No more questions," snapped Duga. "Just do what I tell you and when. If I have to repeat myself again to you…" He nodded to the corpse of the lord.

Staegrim kept his face grim until Duga had turned and stalked away, leaving him standing amongst the slew of dead lords. There had to be maybe twenty or thirty bodies, most of whom had died by Duga's hand, yet it wasn't Duga's prowess with the blade that unnerved Staegrim—he'd seen better warriors than this blue-eyes. Hell, he once did a job for a

Kemen sandseller who could move things with her mind. Between her strange fork-like daggers and her wicked brain, she'd torn a whole regiment of men to pieces in a matter of minutes. She'd paid Staegrim for his time at the end of it all, they went their separate ways, and that was that.

The coin Duga had tossed him was a double header. Staegrim the Feared knew coins. He knew each and every unsmiling face better than he knew his mammy's wrinkled lot, and double headers were as rare as you could ask for. This one mark was minted and pressed before the Bohr occupation, and although it only looked like a two-bit mark, Staegrim could probably have gotten a good bed for the week from it. Men like Duga, men who held in their fists the lives of others, had no idea of the true value of things, even if all he did was speak of honour and value. Staegrim knew about value. Value kept you warm, fed and well-laid, and there was absolutely no value without coins. It *always* came back to coins.

There was always a danger in being a bastard that you'd meet an even bigger bastard. Most who paid for a bastard behaved themselves because when there was something you didn't or couldn't do yourself, you'd get a bastard to do it for you. Bastards were dangerous and loyal to nothing but the coin. Everyone knew that.

"A double header," said Staegrim, chuckling. "Two sides, one coin." He flicked the heavy mark and let it slap against his palm. "Heads. I win."

KAVIK DRAGGED ENOUGH AIR IN HIS LUNGS TO FILL A SKY balloon, but he was still out of breath. He'd ridden hard around the valley to get back to the Tsiorc side, but not so hard that he should feel as though the Forbringr above was stealing his breath. Deep down he knew it was the machine of fear pumping his heart and lungs, but he would not acknowledge it, nor let it best him.

He heeled the dappled yearling forward along the sides of Laeb's butterfly formation. Soldier after soldier, pale-faced and fearful. War took on many forms, but ultimately it all ended the same way, with men and women who had no right being there, meeting their maker. The yearling whinnied at the noises of death, but there was not much to be done about it. The young animal was the only one left alive that could have borne his weight—he would never have ridden her any other time.

"I'm here for the commander," he said, pulling the horse to a stop near a pale, teenage guard.

"Let him through, boy!"

Kavik had never liked Commander Suilven, but not liking a man was no reason not to follow him. "Commander, apologies. I thought Laeb was—"

"What are you even doing here, horse master? Shouldn't someone of your size be fighting alongside your brethren? Seeing as we have no horses or nara left."

Before Kavik could answer Suilven's eyes rolled and he turned away, but one of the officers nodded to him, and Kavik trotted the yearling quietly over to his side.

"Did you see those bombs, Kavik?"

"Aye, I did. The bloody things almost burned the skin right off me. Duga did mention that they would burn hotter than the sun." He lowered his voice. "Where's Laeb?"

The magister adjusted his stiff collar and wiped the rain from his thick grey moustache. "He just...went in. Some balls that one. I'm beginning to wonder if sounding the retreat and then re-establishing our positions was all part of his plan. I blew the horn of my accord because we were ready to fight anew. I made that decision, but that bloody blue-eyes has me questioning even that!"

Kavik scanned the sea of men for Laeb, but from the plateau the rain was just too damn heavy to see anything except the shapes of two armies locked in battle—the Tsiorc a cup and the lords the water filling it.

"There!" Kavik picked out Laeb's slender frame weaving in and out of the front lines between knots of fighting. "He'll get himself killed!"

"You're not wrong," said the magister. "He won't last long in there. But then that's what happens when you ignore your orders. The head chooses, the body acts. As it has been and always will be." The magister slammed the long horn in through his grey nara's strapping. "Bloodied fool."

Laeb was struggling. There were others in there fighting with him—the Tsiorc looked to actually be gaining ground for the first time—but Laeb still looked like he would soon be overcome.

Kavik shook his head. "He's no fool."

"I know what you're thinking, Kavik, but it's suicide. A death path." The magister glanced at the other officers then lowered his voice. "Go fast, otherwise they will try to stop you too."

"May you always fight, Magister."

"And you, Kavik."

Kavik heeled his yearling forward, leaning hard onto the animal's neck. She whinnied in glee as she flew down the hill, and regret touched Kavik's heart at what was likely coming her way.

"LET ME THROUGH!"

The back lines parted quickly, but the inner lines were a different story. They were all focused on the fighting, waiting eagerly for their chance to join the fray. Kavik slowed the yearling, using her weight to shoulder through towards where he'd seen Laeb fighting. The sound of steel on steel grew louder, and from his horse's back, he could see the deaths of the men and women around him clearly. Familiar faces, young faces, too young. Bright blood. Hard steel. Muddied leather. Sweat and fear.

LAEB SWUNG WILDLY; IT WAS ALL AROUND HIM NOW, YET he could do nothing but wait for the victors to emerge from each fight. The reality of battle wasn't anything resembling organisation. It was chaos. And still he found himself in the spaces between, awaiting the bringer of his death. Then she came, emerging from a scuffle with two rebels, both of whom fell to her feet simultaneously. The lord with a helmet of shining black and long horns screamed in his direction. Laeb readied himself, trying to keep his mind clear, but through the thickness a shining memory bloomed like fire...

"DUGA—"

"Fine. You look after yourself if that's what you're so keen to do."

Duga paused briefly to pet a sleeping dog, then vanished behind a street corner. Gods, who would have thought a mountainside could be steep? The streets of Mount Terävä were tight too, not as tight as over the bridge in the white gardens of Vasen, but still, he didn't want to get lost amongst all these shanties. The city of Tyr was a union of extremes, with the rich on one side and the poor on the other, separated by a channel of water called the Way which was fast and wide enough to drown even the strongest swimmers. The bridge may have connected the two sides, but it was a divide as literal as the stone itself.

Laeb remembered every detail of the place as if it was yesterday because this was the place he had met her for the first time. Her skin, *untroubled by time, her clothes, plain but well-made, and her eyes, full of life and wonder. Barely a minute after Duga had left him, she had stepped before him and given him a fleeting scowl. Fleeting because the rest of her crew were on top of Laeb before he could swing a stick, let alone a sword.*

The first thug came in from the left, jumping over the dog and kicking through the air. It might have been comical any other time, but that boot caught Laeb sweet, right across the jaw. The man hit the ground but didn't crumple to a heap, rather he sprang forwards and rolled sideways. Another thug came rushing in, and this one was armed. A strange weapon: two sticks held by a short chain was tucked into his shorts. All the while, she stood behind smirking. Was she waiting her turn to fight a blue-eyes? Or was she the leader, directing thugs like trained dogs?

Laeb reached for his sword.

"Ra!" The second thug was dark-skinned but more importantly three heads taller than Laeb. He held his hands like knives, using them with the same power as a fist, assaulting Laeb's neck and joints, looking for weaknesses. Laeb thrust his free hand out, wishing he'd loaded up on actual knives before leaving the docks.

The blow hit the fighter's cheek, glancing off weakly.

"Och'hai, mur dan!" said the thug, grinning. Laeb smiled back as he slipped his sword out, catching the thug under the nose with the pommel. The man reeled back, then stopped as though the whole thing were a dance. He flourished, mocking Laeb, and then rushed forward. The point of Laeb's sword found the sheath again and the whole thing slid back in.

Fists then.

The first thug, squat but powerful, stood politely waiting for a turn, arms folded and tapping a foot.

"Argh!" Another slap from the big one stung at Laeb's cheek. Retreating, Laeb wracked his brains for something he could use against this beast of a man. His heel caught, and Laeb reached down and grabbed the sleeping dog by the scruff.

"Haha!" said the fighter. "Mur dan ah, courha mus'd iaa?"

The dog, rabid with anger snarled behind Laeb's hand.

"I don't speak the common tongue!"

And that's when she finally stepped in. He would never forget that moment, her pale skin and red hair glowing in the bright moonlight. She was a freedom fighter, like the rest of these ragged fools, but by the gods, she was utterly, utterly beguiling.

"Walking Terävä at sundown," she said smoothly in Daliaen. "Alone? Unable to speak the language?" She jumped back as the dog snapped at her.

"Now, now," said Laeb. "Is this how all Terävaeans treat guests?"

"Guests?" spat the woman. "You are no guest here. How did you get into our city? The docks? Like every other damned blue-eyes around here! The city is filled with them. Isn't that right, Pols?"

Pols grunted. Arms still folded, but as tense as a broken mattress.

She was being coy. "You're playing games with me. Don't do that."

She smiled, impressed. "I play games, blue-eyes. It's what I do. But you're right. I hold no grudge to the migrants of Sulitar."

"I also like to play games."

"What gave me away?"

"A migrant shouting about migrants? How old were you when you came here?"

The woman's eyes narrowed. "Pols, what do you make of this one then?"

Pols frowned. "You tell me. Apparently you're best pals now. You promised us a fight." The woman shot him a glare. "Fine. He might be handy with a sword, if he knew how to pull it from his sheath."

"And which end to use," added the big one, touching his fat lip gingerly.

"So, we are all freedom fighters," said Laeb. "But who do you fight for?"

"We fight for ourselves," said the woman. "For all of us. For you, for Terävaeans, for New Bakla, for Nord."

"New Bakla? So, that's where you're from. I see it now." He looked her up and down. *"The sun must have been cruel to one as fair as you."*

She gestured to the two fighters, then made a sign with her fingers. The big one rolled his eyes, but Pols kept his glare hard. He said something in Tyrian and stalked off, shaking his head.

"You must trust them if they're happy to leave you with someone so dangerous." The dog growled again, and Laeb let it go. The thing didn't run away but rather turned and started snapping at Laeb's heels. His hand dropped to his hilt.

"So, you cannot win against our, what did you call them, freedom fighters, but you'll happily dispatch a helpless street dog?" She pulled a wrapped packet from her pocket, and the dog's ears pricked at the sound of rustling paper. *"Here. Here, look!"* She threw a pink sweet bouncing away down the street, and the dog bolted after it.

"Thank you," said Laeb.

"Twice, I've saved your life now," she said, licking her fingers. *And you owe me another maechi. Three actually. One for the dog and one each for Pols and Crohmt."*

"And where might one buy maechi?"

"There's a stall near the bar where I work."

"The docks? What a coincidence..."

LAEB'S SWORD WAS COMPLETELY USELESS. AN AXE WOULD have served him better, but there was nothing he could do about it now. He batted away another wayward attack as best he could, stumbling himself against the wall of steaming, leather-clad soldiers. The fighting was close now, and many were resorting to hand-to-hand combat, lifting helmets, gouging eyes and fish hooking—a dirty fight. A dagger plunged towards him, but there was nowhere to retreat to. The lead guard Laeb had ridden with reappeared within an almost impossible gap, his black plait bouncing on his shoulder, and caught the dagger scratching wildly at Laeb's armoured stomach. He twisted the arm on the end of it, and the weapon splatted into the mud, followed shortly by the man. His screams were cut short as the soldier was trampled.

Laeb's own feet slid, but the guard's arm was there again. "Thank you..."

"It's Cashiq, Captain!" shouted the guard. He thrust a short sword into Laeb's hand. "Use this!"

The fighting swallowed Cashiq, and they were separated again as two lovers parting. Laeb spotted a pocket of space and slid into it, desperately trying to move back into the safety of Tsiorc lines—this was no place for him, not unless he truly intended to kill. The gods had at least spared him the need so far. Cashiq's calm expression was visible briefly to Laeb's left as he cut down anyone who dared come close. He may as well have been felling trees.

The lord soldier with the black horned helmet slid into the pocket as Cashiq had and wasted no time in attacking. "Thought you'd lost me, eh?" Sprinting hard, she leapt at him out of the mess of bodies, hiding something—

Her axe cut through the air a maker of makers ready to cut deep into him. Laeb threw himself out of its way, cursing himself for not seeing the deception. The axe came hurtling back towards him in a reverse arc. She was easily half his weight, but she knew where to focus the weight of that malicious weapon, and the shining axe-head glanced by his cheek, a finger's breadth distant. The gods were testing him now. He could wield his bluesteel sword better than most, though perhaps not as well as Duga, but in here he was as disposable as any other. He had to think outside of his box.

He waited for the next slew of swings, raising Cashiq's shortsword as if to meekly fend them off. The lord soldier saw his weakness and took the bait, starting the set of moves that would likely end with a horizontal swipe to his guts. The moment came, as it did for all, and she twisted the handle of that huge axe, flattening the blade to change its direction. Laeb dropped the shortsword to the mud, stepped forward and punched the soldier hard in the face. Pain blossomed on his knuckles and wrist, but he'd caught enough of her to knock her off balance. She reeled, and the momentum of her swing threw her weak side to him. He brought a heavy elbow into her opposite shoulder, dislocating it, the lord soldier struggled back and Laeb retreated, spinning and grabbing the sword.

Before his grip had even finished tightening, she stepped forward and jabbed Laeb in the face with the top of her axe. Metal cracked teeth. Salt and blood.

The lord smiled with an equally bloody mouth and rolled her dislocated shoulder back into joint. "Always wanted to bag myself a captain," she said, spitting blood. "Even a pussy-small one like you."

Laeb tried to concentrate on the words, but his head was thick. The moment was so far and away from himself that if not for his body, he was barely here at all...

He remembered the fragrance of her mingling with the sweet in her hand, the fresh scent of fish and sea. Smells that drew together like physical clouds that could be touched. He didn't realise it at the time, but each of those smells would imprint on his mind as they stood at the docks together, and many times after.

"You coming in?"

The Fiskar was as far away from a bar as a rowboat is from a Sulitarian ocean vessel. It had eight stools and a space for preparation barely large enough for one, and yet the woman and the owner danced around each other, taking ingredients for meals and bringing them together in huge bowls. He watched her for some time before the owner appeared in front, frowning through long, matted locks.

"Are you eating?"

Laeb shook his head. He was starving, and the cooking smells clinging to him were not helping. "I'm not hungry."

"Forbringr's Blood. Then why's he here, eh, Fia?"

"Fia? The freedom fighter?"

"It's Atalfia. No one calls me Fia. Not even Allander here. You got that, old man?"

Allander mumbled something behind her, but it was lost amongst all the slurping and bowl scraping.

The beads hanging over the door rustled, and three Kumpani floated in. Their conversation drifted between hand signals, nods, and the occasional word so that even the most astute follower would have no idea of the subject. They sat down, ignoring everyone in the room, as was the Kumpani way. Some called them escorts, but not more than once. He had heard of the great respect held for the Kumpani in the cities above the Hätärian borders, but in truth this was his first actual sight of them. They were beautiful, but they were keen too, judging by their opinions on the Kael of Tyr.

"You know, it strikes me," said Laeb, as Atalfia placed a steaming cup in front of him, "that your friends on the street—"

"Not friends."

Laeb smirked. "Not paid either though."

Atalfia's big eyes studied his face as he spoke. All at once, he felt alone, like she was the predator and he the prey. She was perfect. "They are fighters of freedom. As you say."

"I could say a great many things."

"And I bet you do."

Laeb took a sip from the cup. It was sweet and delicious with tiny blue flowers floating in it. "And what freedoms need fought for here exactly?"

Atalfia frowned. "You seem to be under the illusion that we don't need to fight here?"

Laeb tipped back the hot seete down his throat. "Tyr does okay. Doesn't it?"

"Does it?" She tilted her head. "Is it the people sleeping in the

31

streets that do okay? Or perhaps those forced to beg for scraps at the Domst. The razor monkeys eat better than the dock workers. Men and women who spend every minute of the day fishing, watched by their lords in case they feel the urge to swallow a live squid just to keep hunger at bay for another day." She grabbed the cup and refilled it from a steel kettle. "You know, when I came to this city, things were doing okay. I could move freely across the bridge without being questioned, I could choose which work suited me best, be it tying ropes, washing decks, working in a tailors in the market, even building homes in Vasen. A group of us rendered the entire east wall in white and oh! We were paid so well for it. But it doesn't take much for a regime to change. The Bohr have always been here, there. Watching. Waiting. One day everything is fine, and the next we are tumbling from the knife-edge in the wrong direction." She waited for a response, but Laeb gave none. "Does that sound okay?"

"It sounds like you know what you're about."

She studied him again. "I do." She slammed the empty soup bowls down. "And we decided to do something about it!"

Laeb should have had something to say, something witty. Maybe the seete's syrupy alcohol was dulling his senses.

"There are twenty of us now." She placed three cups in front of the Kumpani, who didn't acknowledge her.

Allander danced around her to grab a jar of old leaves and accidentally bumped against her. They shared a look. The barman might have been simply telling her to not be so free with her tongue—Laeb could be anyone after all—or he might have just been annoyed that she was talking more than working. Whichever it was, it didn't seem to Laeb that the owner of this fine establishment was a part of whatever cause this woman fought for.

A rustle of wind blew in from the doorway and a hand took Laeb's shoulder...

.   .   .

THE LORD SOLDIER TURNED ON HER HEEL AS IF SHE WAS going to run, and instinctively Laeb sprang forward. She stopped, moving awkwardly to the left and then to the right, spinning on the spot. That axe would be following soon after, it had to be—the tiny woman had to use pivots and fulcrums to move that heavy weapon. Laeb held up his shortsword, ready to block, but the attack came from the other side. The axe pole burrowed deep into his guts knocking the wind out of him and sending him to the dirt.

"Argh!"

She stood above him, mocking him. Turning the axe in her hand. "Lucky, lucky, lucky, Captain! Next time I'll be sure to use the sharp side."

Her expression twisted and she flew up into the air, impossibly high right over Laeb's head, landing in a broken heap behind him. In her place stood a horse and rider.

"You all right, Captain?"

"Kavik. Thank the sea, sun, and stars! Help me up." Kavik's thick arms drew Laeb up like a newborn to his father. "It's good to see you, Kavik. Good timing."

"Aye well, it seems your luck has taken you this far, but don't be expecting it to last much longer standing about in this tearing mess. Come on."

Laeb was offering a nod of thanks when the spear skewered Kavik's horse, pinning it to the ground and sending them both back to the mud.

The Bohr was probably one of the smallest he'd seen but it was still thickly muscled, with a set of horns that curled down past its pointed ears to a wide, grimacing mouth.

A smile split its face. "Captain," snarled the Bohr.

In its claw was the remnants of a Tsiorc banner, the triangle-cross sigil painted roughly across the canvas in black. The Bohr let the flag fall to the mud, then it was pouncing towards him, running on all fours like a wolf. Laeb leapt to

33

the side, but the Bohr was too quick, and it countered and slashed out. Pain bit into Laeb's stomach where four neat gashes had sliced through the thick leather.

Kavik jumped as the Bohr spun around, barely avoiding being cut to pieces himself. He pulled a sword from his belt—clumsily, the way a man who spent his days murmuring in horses' ears rather than training, might. Kavik was the heaviest man Laeb knew—the bones of a giant, the man would say—but even his bulk was eclipsed as the Bohr stood to his full height between them. Kavik's sword shook, but it wasn't the blade that took the Bohr in the guts. Kavik's broken horse gave one final kick and knocked the Bohr back, crushing the lines of lords behind.

Kavik's sword no longer shook. Anger replaced fear, but it was short-lived. The Bohr charged again, and this time Laeb had no choice but to meet it. He rushed forward, swinging his shortsword. It sang through the air, then clashed against the Bohr's heavy forearms and glanced off. The Bohr batted away his weapon and back-handed Laeb across the face, knocking him tumbling to the mud.

Laeb tried to push himself up, feeling flag canvas beneath his fingers, but the ground lurched beneath him. Ringing filled his ears; the world was on its side, but a part of his addled brain was able to follow the ensuing fight as Kavik wrestled with the Bohr. The Keeper of Horses dropped between its legs and punched up into the balls of the thing, then he was climbing onto its back, stabbing and clutching at the Bohr's neck.

"UP!"

Cashiq's face appeared, and Laeb was on his feet again, unsteady and with a thick feeling of spew in his stomach. The guard nodded, then joined the fight, slashing, cutting, dipping, ducking. The Bohr roared in frustration as the two little men ran circles round him, cutting at his ankles, behind the knee, between the legs.

It swung out wildly, but those haymakers were as predictable as the creature's downfall. Its strength was waning. Kavik, his muscles straining, pinned the Bohr's arm behind its back, forcing the creature to its knees. Emboldened, Cashiq ducked under a wild grab, right up to the Bohr's chest and plunged his sword in through the kidneys. The Bohr should have roared in pain, it should have shouted at the sky, denying the gods before it met them face-to-face, but it didn't. The Bohr smiled.

In one motion, it freed its arm from Kavik's grip, launching the man into the air, then grabbed Cashiq's head. Cashiq screamed as the Bohr's bear claws burst through the skin on his face and scalp, but he was still able to reach out with his dagger and slice the Bohr's face from forehead to chin. It was the last blood he would ever spill.

"You did well to find me in here, Duga," said Laeb. "And how is it that you are able to avoid disturbing even hanging beads? That is a trick I should wish for you to show me one day."

Duga's mottled face was expressionless as he spoke, he truly was a man who gave nothing away. "We are all set, Captain."

Laeb pushed up from the bar and replaced the stool. One of the Kumpani looked over at him, painted eyelids fluttering. Apparently the title had not gone unnoticed. "Good luck to you and your twenty, Atalfia."

The freedom fighter's eyes darted back and forth between him and the Kumpani, then narrowed. "And you. Captain. Until we meet again."

The night was deliciously cool, the chill wind even giving the occasional relief from the odour of raw fish. It wasn't a smell Laeb disliked, far from it—it reminded him of home, and if there was ever

MICHAEL S. JACKSON

a time to be reminded of the familiar, it was here in Tyr—but the chill took him back to the helm of a ship. Sulitar was an island continent, but it had never lost its connection to the Middle Sea. Brine in the blood, they called it.

Laeb followed Duga over the cobbles to the harbour edge, and a familiar figure turned towards him from the deck of an Anqamorian vessel.

"Dia'slar, old friend!"

"Laeb, is that you?" Dia'slar shut the ledger in his hand, and leapt down from deck to dock. "You look skinny," he said, shaking Laeb's hand. "How I don't miss that life."

"Yes, well. Just make sure you don't get too comfortable here, Dia'slar. You'll be munching on burned rat and bitter potatoes soon enough."

Dia'slar grinned. "How could I be comfortable around these... things? After all they took from us. From Bryn."

Laeb drew a ragged breath. Since fleeing their home and landing here, they had lost much. But here they were, rebels standing in the centre of Tyr, the Bohr's stronghold. It was bittersweet, though, to be amongst so much wealth and food whilst his own men went hungry.

"We'll never forget the reasons, Dia'slar." Laeb gripped Dia'slar's hand tightly.

Dia'slar nodded. "Never, my friend. How are the numbers looking now?"

Duga spoke first. "A ton."

Dia'slar's eyebrows arched again. "Good progress."

Laeb hated himself for the swell of pride he felt, but Dia'slar was a hard man to please.

"These Hätärian towns have lost many to the Bohr," said Duga. "The flatlands leave nowhere to hide."

"What of the mountains?" Asked Dia'slar, folding his arms around the ledger.

Duga shook his head. "These are families. Hätär's mountains are a week's walk from the Way, even on a good horse. And these are simple folks. But their blood is strong, and they fight."

"Even so close to the Kemen border? After generations of losses?"

"Especially so. They will join the core of our army."

"Wonderful. So, where to next? West into Anqamor? I know someone at Raven's Torr who could ferry you over the channel there."

"You know someone who could hide a thousand soldiers?" said Laeb. "And transport them over the sea?"

"Indeed," said Dia'slar. "It would be expensive, but she would do it if I asked."

"I bet she would. But as tempting as Anqamor is, it's a dead end for us. We need solid ground beneath our feet." Laeb took a long breath. "Dali. We're moving into Dali."

"North?"

"And then into Nord itself."

Dia'slar scoffed. "Laeb, I hardly think—" His expression softened, and his gaze rolled beyond Laeb's shoulder. "Hardly think the moonsquid will be out for another month yet. Oh, and who is this?"

Atalfia walked up to him, taking them all in and ignoring Dia'slar's lingering stare. "You forgot to pay."

"Pay?" said Laeb.

Atalfia crossed her arms. "Pay. When you drink something, you pay for it. I would have thought even a captain would know such a thing. Allander is not best pleased. You should be happy I stand before you and not him."

"Oh, I am."

Dia'slar stepped towards her, but she didn't budge, nor did she acknowledge the man towering over her. "You'll have to forgive my brother here..." His expressive face dipped in and out of expectation as he waited for her name. It was a game, Laeb was sure, that had worked for him many times before.

"Her name is Atalfia," said Laeb, after a long minute. "She leads a band of freedom fighters. Rough lads, but not too bright."

"Sounds perfect for you then. Take down those names, eh, Duga?"

"Are you going to pay or not?" said Atalfia, her eyes never leaving Laeb's.

Laeb dipped into his pocket and pulled a Sulitarian mark from the open bag within. He held it out, and when Atalfia reached out to take it, he took her hand. "I am a captain. A tactician for a rebel force called the Tsiorc. We, too, are fighting. We fight the Bohr."

Dia'slar jerked this way and that to see who could be listening among the dock workers, but it was Duga who spoke first. "Captain?" he said, wearing a look of confusion. "What are you—?"

"We are currently stationed on the south side of Hätär," continued Laeb, "awaiting passage across the Way. You see, there is a narrow channel smugglers often use to move between the north and south, and it is our intention to cross with our one thousand soldiers so we may bolster our forces in Dali."

Duga's hand once again lay upon Laeb's shoulder. "Captain, we don't know this woman or anyone with whom she fights with."

Dia'slar nodded, his expression serious for the first time. "It's not often I would agree with Duga, but you'd do well to be cautious with your words here, Laeb."

"Well, that's just it, isn't it?" said Laeb, flatly. "They're my words. A captain's words."

"Laeb—"

Duga shook his head and stepped between them all, splitting the group and leading Dia'slar away to the ship. Laeb kept his glare hard until both men were gone from view on the deck.

"He trusts you," said Atalfia.

"He does. But he just doesn't trust you. Yet."

"Yet?"

"As strong as the Tsiorc are, Atalfia. We need help. The Bohr are too strong to face without numbers. One on one, we have no chance, but as a force...a united force could take over and dismantle their regime forever. Imagine a human government within Tyr. How long has it been? A hundred cycles? Two hundred?"

"A hundred and forty-six. Why are you telling me this?"

"We need friends in the cities, Atalfia. Voices we can count upon."
And there it was, it was out. His big idea. It had come to him barely a
second after he had first seen her, and now it was no longer an idea,
but a proposition.

"You want me to spy for you?"

Laeb shook his head. "The Tsiorc are not freedom fighters. We
fight to keep what is already ours. Freedom implies we are caged. We
were here first, Atalfia. Us. Not them. They have no more right to
take our world from us than they do our lives." He pulled back,
leaving more than a Sulitarian mark in her possession.

"But how?"

"Dia'slar will get you started. He can introduce you to our
network here within Tyr, and he will help you infiltrate even the
highest echelons of the Bohr's government."

Atalfia looked dumbfounded, but it was clear the words had
landed and taken seed. The argument was as simple and straightfor-
ward as the sun and the sky. As bright and cold as an autumn day. It
was why he had chosen her. It was why he had ventured through the
streets of Terävä in the dead of night. It was why he had left the
Fiskar without paying. It was why he had loitered here, in sight of
the bar upon the dock of Terävä, waiting patiently for her to
accost him.

"How on earth am I supposed to infiltrate a government? What
do I have other than fifteen fighters to rely upon?"

"Fifteen?"

"Twelve." She licked her lips then sighed long and hard. "Fine, it's
seven. Or at least it will be. Soon."

Laeb shook his head. "Atalfia. I don't want you to fight. I want
you to watch, to study and observe. Wherever there are Bohr making
decisions for the people of Tyr, there will be you and Dia'slar
following."

"But how?"

He nodded over at the Fiskar's entrance, and Atalfia turned. The
three Kumpani had just stepped out through the beads. They carried

on talking in signs, unaware that Atalfia and Laeb were watching them.

"*I'm sure you'll find a way. Fia.*"

THE BOHR'S FIST CLOSED WITH A SICKENING CRUNCH, THEN the beast was tossing Cashiq's body away. Kavik stepped back, his face pale with fear. Laeb's legs shook, the burning wound at his stomach forgotten.

The Bohr brought a terrible claw to his face and etched a rune there—red blood against yellow skin. "What an honour," growled the Bohr, "to be killed by Mat'orza. His strength belongs to me."

The pocket of space was larger now, its walls a ring of battle weathered soldiers, their own fights stopped or at least paused to watch as this Bohr tore Laeb and Kavik to pieces. Someone started banging their shield, a Tsiorc shield. Then another and another. Those weathered faces began to look familiar to Laeb. There was Liam, tall, skinny, and as hard as rock. Rothmarr stood next to him, looking barely twenty even though he was older than Laeb. And Orst, a veteran guard and Sulitarian fighter Laeb had first met in Tyr. Orst was one of the few who looked like he wanted to be here, and the old scars upon his weathered skin certainly gave him every right to be.

Every face was a Tsiorc soldier, and Laeb knew them all, had trained with them, led them. A slow realisation crossed the Bohr's stupid animal face as the shield-banging grew louder. It stepped into the middle of the circle, snarling, barking, biting at the air. It swiped madly at the ring but met only a wall of shields. Steel flashed as each soldier ran in to meet the Bohr. A young woman, slim and who looked barely able to hold a sword, darted in under the Bohr's legs and cut through the tendons on its reverse ankles, which pinged away from the beast's legs. She rolled away from the Bohr's wild retaliation. Dropping to its knees, the Bohr roared to the sky, as soldier after soldier jumped upon its back, stabbing and cutting. Liam stepped up to it, savouring the every second, until finally, and with a mighty roar, Liam swiped his longsword in a huge arc and cut the Bohr's head from its shoulders. It fell, sprawling across the Tsiorc flag.

"MAY YOU ALWAYS FIGHT!" roared Liam, his sword held high. The Tsiorc soldiers roared the same, exalting in their victory.

Before Laeb could get caught up in it, Orst appeared. "We've bought ourselves some time, Cap, but our flanks are being stretched thin." He spat a wad of blood across the dead Bohr's back. "Cashiq, may he always fight, wanted me to tell you that the front lines are being pushed too far. Our wings are being clipped, Cap!"

Laeb drew what breath he could. "The butterfly will hold, Orst. Are the lines rotating?"

Orst shook his head. "No. They either can't or don't know how to."

"Orst, I need you and the other guards to pull the wings in tighter. The flanks must stay strong, or the bulk of our soldiers will be exposed, and this battle will be over."

Orst looked conflicted. "Cap, this battle is long lost. There are a few pockets like this one, but we are the losers here. The lords are too many. The Bohr are all but dead, but the holes they have rent in our lines are not easily filled again. We simply do not have the numbers, Cap. The bottleneck will fail—"

"The bottleneck will hold!" Laeb caught himself, sparing a glance for the commander and the rest of the officers standing upon the brow of the hill above. "If we lose this battle, Orst, the Tsiorc die here today. We must not let that happen. It might be that in the face of the gods, our actions will be pointless, but we will fight until every last breath has left us. The bottleneck must hold." He took Orst by the shoulders. "For Cashiq, for our families, for all humans of Rengas, it must hold."

STAEGRIM'S GAZE RAKED OVER THE BODIES, SEARCHING FOR movement. He was good at seeing things that were not in their place, although when you stood upon a field of dead soldiers, order was not something often found.

"Forbringr's blood, hurry it up, you shite!"

Qor looked up at him, her hand stuck in the leather pockets of a lord. "Why? Do you see him?"

"Just hurry it up."

Qor ripped her hand from the lord's armour, pocketed the contents, then hurried over, keeping low.

"There's no one here." He spun on the spot. "No one here...no one...here..."

"Don't play the fool, Stae. You look enough like one anyway with that ridiculous coat." She covered a nostril and blew snot out of the other. "None of this is going to help us with Duga now, is it?"

"It's a jacket, not a coat, you utter shite."

"There's no fucking diff—"

"There's a huge fucking difference! See these buttons, they come down to the hip, not the balls. And this material is much lighter than what you might find on...what? Are you laughing?"

Qor pressed her lips together so hard the colour was almost completely drained from them. She looked like a corpse.

Staegrim shook his head. "You're dicking with me. Great. Thank you."

"Well, why not? Why'd you call me over?"

"I did no such thing. I said hurry up."

"You said hurry it up, *you shite*," added Qor.

Staegrim chuckled. "Well, you are a shite. A giant, sewer-clogging shite."

Qor closed her eyes. "Stae, where is Duga?"

"Where we left him. He gave us our leave to scavenge the dead, so we politely acquiesced."

"I thought he would, yunno, want to be a part of it."

Stae laughed heartily at that. There really was nothing like a good laugh to get the blood pumping. "Qor. My dearest. The high-ups don't take part in the dirty work. He got us here behind enemy lines to perform the task. His job is over. He threw a mask on and disappeared as soon as he could. You saw it."

"I did. But I thought he might be coming back." Before Staegrim could reply, Qor rolled her eyes and beat him to it. "Yes, yes. We're here to do a job. I get it. Do we even know where this *Kael* is?"

"Yes. Now listen." Staegrim dug into his coin purse. It was in that pocket where there shouldn't be a pocket. He thanked Morlak's wonderful sewing fingers silently again for that one. "How much did Duga give you?"

"Four marks," said Qor. "I found twenty bits from this lot though."

"Four?" said Staegrim. "He gave me ten."

Qor stomped her foot. "Ten! That fucker. I should find him and—"

Staegrim shook his head. "He'll only cut you a new arsehole."

"Well, fuck." She started looking all shifty-like. "Give me three of yours."

Staegrim sighed. He had seen it coming a hundred leagues off, and still he had to quell the immediate sickening in his stomach at the thought of giving away his money. Still, the price was worth it in this case. "Piss off."

Qor's eyebrows danced. "Two then. Just for the shit you've given me so far."

Staegrim grimaced. "So, you're telling me I have to pay to work with you now, is that it!?"

"Don't shit on me, Stae. Two is a fair price. We agreed a half-split when we met that prick in Drakemyre, plus whatever we get for afters." Qor bared her yellow teeth. "My counting tells me you're currently three heavier than you should be."

Staegrim prepared himself for the lie. He had to get it just right. Qor was a liar the same as he. Any holes in this, and he would be a partner down again, if she didn't just stick him through first.

"You're right," he said, calmly. "Two is fair, especially seeing as we're off the hook now."

"Off the hook? Already? We've not bled this Kael yet!"

Staegrim schooled his face into sadness and let the lie flow from his lips. "Duga told me just before he disappeared that we're not to make the kill. Something to do with the master plan, I guess." He let the false words sit between them for the briefest spell—it had to be perfect, but there also had to be some truth to it too. The best lies were always woven against the truth. "This Laeb, the famous tactician making all of these ridiculous moves."

"Like the dead animals."

"And those bombs. Well, he doesn't know we're even here. I overheard Duga telling Kavik not to mention our little collaboration. The thing is though, I suspect this Laeb..." He opened his hands urging Qor to participate.

"Is the one who pays us."

Staegrim nodded slowly. "Which means we don't get our

final cut." And there it was. It was really quite beautiful. Like poetry. He should have been an actor.

"And he calls us the bastards!" Qor shook her head. "What sort of cunt backs off on a deal? The piece of shit! I'm going to find him and stick him through!"

"Qor, Qor...You'll just get yourself killed. He gave me two options. He said you either fight for the Tsiorc or he would kill us both right there."

"He said that?" Qor frowned, a hint of doubt speckling her brow. "When?"

He pulled three coins from his purse. "Look, take the three. That at least makes us square now." Qor looked like she might question him further, until at last, her dirty finger-nails raked over his palm.

"Done," she said. "No takebacks."

"No takebacks."

Qor almost tripped on a dead lord at her feet, the very same that had nearly caved in Staegrim's head with a mace. She put the boot in him. "Well, what now? Where the hell do we go now, Stae?"

Staegrim kept the smile away from his face with the greatest of efforts. "Now? Now we go and see if the lords need a hand. Seems there might still be some milk we can sup from that cow."

"You want to ask the Kael if we can help him win this battle?"

Qor was young. She'd been shadowing Staegrim for some time now. Had it been ten cycles already? "You remember when we met, Qor? Back in Drakemyre. I'd just travelled up from the Snake's Belly in Anqamor and I'd spent the day with a seer. Robbed him blind, or at least I think I did. It gets a bit fuzzy around then."

Qor nodded. "I remember it."

"Aye, well. You learned a lesson that day. And many since. Thing is, Qor. We can leave here rich, or we can leave poor."

"You left rich that day, from what I recall." Qor ran a hand through her hair. "Well. It has to be rich, doesn't it?"

"And unless you want to spend the rest of the day rummaging through the pockets of those poorer than you, I guess that means we switch sides. We join the lord's army."

Qor shook her head. "I don't know, Stae, that fella Duga... He makes me nervous."

"You wanted to stick him like a pig not four seconds ago! Well, now's your chance!"

"Yeh," she said, "but he's dangerous. And sly. I doubt I'd get even a little close to him before he lopped my head off."

Staegrim nodded. "That's because he used to be a bastard. I know it in my bones. Only a bastard knows a bastard, and he knows bastards."

"Stop saying *bastard*, Stae."

"Fine. But you know what? Let's not make a choice when we don't have to. Let's give the Forbringr herself, the Mother, the chooser of choices, the last say." He pulled Duga's double header coin from his pocket. He knew the feel of it against the rest, so it was easy enough. He flashed it in front of Qor's eyes too fast to see, then placed it on his poised thumb. "Heads says we march right up to the Kael and ask to join the Bohr and his lords, tails says we stay right here with the Tsiorc rebels until something better comes along. Fair?"

He tossed the coin.

THE BOHR'S CAMP WAS AS OSTENTATIOUS AS ANY STAEGRIM has ever seen. The tents were all thick, handstitched canvas, nice stuff, too, with flashings and silks and banners. The guards all wore burnished steel with not a scratch to be seen in the same shades of grey festooned about the place. The two Panguards standing either side of the main officer's tent stood out amongst all, though, given their lack of steel armour. Giants they were, with nothing but loincloths to cover what Staegrim imagined had to be the biggest cocks that existed on any battlefield. He stepped nervously towards them, led by the two senior soldiers who had disarmed them further down the hill.

Qor glanced sidelong at him. "I want my fucking sword back."

Staegrim shook his head as one of the Pans frowned a furrow surely deep enough to get lost in. "Bastards aren't street dogs." he hissed. "Sometimes you have to talk some. It's not all about killing."

"And my knives."

Staegrim suppressed a sigh. Maybe he was out of his depth here. Maybe this was a stupid idea. That was the problem with lies, they sat atop of each other like dead cows, stinking and rotten, and you had to remember each one regardless of what it looked like. He spared a look for the battlefield itself, two armies locked into a mess of knots and shapes, all trying to best each other. From this height though, it was all too clear that the rebels were fiercely outnumbered. Still, he'd seen plenty of battles turn around at the last minute, and with that talented tactician at the helm, this could easily be one of them.

The animal eyes of the Panguards followed Staegrim and Qor all the way to the command tent on the cusp of the hill. Of all the tents, this was surely the nicest. It smelled of incense and honey even before they stepped inside. The flaps dropped behind them, and the odours assaulted Staegrim's nostrils. He reached for his collar, and something touched his back.

"Don't. Move."

A pair of twins stood there, all gold-plated steel armour and gemstone hilts. Brother and sister, by the looks of their pale white hair.

"It's all right," came a voice from within the haze. "I can manage."

A figure emerged—apparently this tent was so large it had corners. The man, if you could call him that, stood tall, though not as tall as the Panguards. He was Bohr, that much was very clear; his ears were pointed, but he had facial hair, which was unusual for his type, and it was groomed to a tiny plait and bound with a gold ring. His stance was less animalistic, and his features were much more...human.

"You are a Bohr?"

"A Child. A half-blood. As impure and unquantifiable as the space between the moon and the sun. And a very busy one at that. Although, I will accommodate you briefly. I like a good bastard. That is, of course, providing that you are...good."

"The best!" blurted Qor.

"Glad to hear it," said the Kael.

Staegrim cleared his throat. "Kael, it is an honour to meet you. I am Staegrim. Staegrim the Feared."

"The Feared?" The Kael's eyebrows rose a hair. "A named man. Then the honour is mine."

Staegrim lowered his eyes at the Kael's sarcasm. Impertinence would do him no good here.

"And what about you?" said the Kael. "Are you *named,* as it were?"

"I am Qor."

"But of course you are." The Kael looked down at them both, amused. "Please call me Rathe. Kael Rathe. Well, now that we have the formalities out of the way, what is it that you want?"

"Want?" asked Staegrim.

"Yes," said the Kael, impatiently. "I am fighting a battle here. I'm told you sauntered up through vale, the very vale we are currently fighting in. Slipping past three thousand good fighting men is no mean feat. So, as to your want, I am very interested. Very interested indeed."

"Our want," said Staegrim, "is simply to help, sorry, aid the lords' army."

"Aid?" said the Kael. "And how do you intend to aid us? We're doing quite well as it is. Or haven't you been watching?"

Staegrim nodded, he had been prepared for this. "Well, we've been sort of, busy."

"Busy..."

Qor moved to speak, and Staegrim hurried on. "Yes, busy Kael. Very busy. We were in the thick of the action you see."

"Killed a fair few, so we did."

Staegrim closed his eyes in annoyance—Qor would undo this plan very quickly if he did not think fast. "That's right, as bastards we have much experience. We know how to view the battlefield as a whole. A sort of...understanding of what's going on." The Kael frowned at his gestures, but he powered on. "You see, Kael, there's an awful lot you can't see from up here. The smell of blood, the look of fear. Men and women fighting for their lives. 'Cept o'course the lords aren't fighting for their lives. They're here like we're here. For the coin." He was channelling the good stuff now. Rathe's expression had turned from amusement to frowning interest. It was an awkward place to be, but on his mammy's name, he had to get this right. When you walked with lions, you had to be careful you weren't eaten.

"And those who fight for the coin are workers. They buy and sell, but their trade is—"

"Your time is running low, bastard," growled the Kael.

Staegrim drew a long breath, but Qor beat him to it. "We have information about the other side. The rebels."

"What sort of information, Qor?"

Qor clutched at the well-worn leather where her belt knife usually sat. "Well—"

"Well," said Staegrim, standing taller. "Information is a commodity, like any other." Rathe stepped back but those sharp eyes never left his. Staegrim suppressed a smile—negotiation was the same however high you stood in the world. "We're but simple bastards, Kael, but everything has a price. We need to buy food to eat, green to smoke. Qor here has eight children. I myself have two wives back home in Anqamor who wish to bleed me dry."

"Fucking Anqamor," snapped the Kael. "An island of thieves and shipmen! Why did you leave such a *prosperous* place then? Tell me that?" He turned to walk away. "I think our time is up."

It was time to toss the coin. "The Tsiorc are all here now. All of them. Every single one of them. There is not a single one left anywhere else in Rengas."

The weight of the words hung heavy, and it was a long few seconds before Rathe finally spoke. "There are no others?" he said quietly. Qor stared at Staegrim, equally dumbfounded.

"None. They came here to die, and you could be the one to wipe them all out."

Rathe began to pace. "The end of the Tsiorc?" He stopped as a thought seemed to occur to him. "Why would you tell me this? Why, by the great dunes of the wastes, would you come here in the midst of the battle to tell me this? What have you to gain?"

Staegrim chuckled. The power had shifted back to him, but he still had to tread carefully. "We aim to follow, but we aim to win. And *you* are going to win, Kael Rathe. Your paid army may not have the heart of the rebels, but what does heart matter when you outnumber them ten to one."

"Two to one," said the Kael.

"What?"

The Kael held up two fingers. "The lord's army outnumber the rebels two to one."

"Two?" Staegrim's heart leapt. That was high-level information. Officer material. Rathe was going to accept him and Qor into the lord's ranks!

It would mean the beginning of a more official arrangement. Finally, Staegrim might be able to buy a place of his own. A house, or a terrace in Vasen. He'd heard that was the rich side, where all of the wealth of Tyr resided. There were stories of the women too, not just street whores, but women who you could pay to be with you, as a partner, for life. All you needed was coin. It always came back to coin. He would open a shop, like Morlak's but with far nicer cloth. There were merchants from Port Ataska who—

Blood splattered against Staegrim's face and neck, warm and salty. Qor looked as shocked as he must have, but aside from the paleness, her complexion was still as smooth and young as the day he had first met her.

This was someone's home? How could four people use so much space? The walls were of a thick, red stone, quarried from somewhere other than Dali, which alone spoke of the wealth of the place. Who cares about what bloody stones their house was built from? Staegrim moved into the pantry, keeping low. The markets were all in session, so it was doubtful he'd run into someone here, but by the damned Forbringr and her raging blood, it wouldn't do well to have to kill someone, least of all in their own home. He pocketed a small pig pie and stuffed another one in his mouth.

"That's a good pie."" he said, blowing crumbs. Apparently even

the pigs knew how to live it up here in the Halven Estates. The pantry had two doors, so he closed the entrance and left via the other. Another room greeted him, smelling of money. The clean tang of gold hanging in the air was wonderous, one of the finest smells to draw in. He followed it over to the corner, where stood a statue of Mother Baeivi, the Forbringr herself, nursing a baby. He ran a finger over the shining metal, wondering what it would look like in the bright sunshine.

"How many coins will you make, dear Mother?"

He took her raised arm and tried to lift it. No dice. It must have weighed as much as his own mammy, blessed be her shadow. He tried again, and the floor squeaked. Of all the treasures to find, and of all the treasures to leave behind. He made a fist around the statue's raised arm and twisted as hard as he could until the thing bent. Poor Mother. Twist again. Again. AGAIN. Finally, she gave it to him, a broken arm of pure gold.

"I'll be back for the rest of you some other day, dear Mother."

"You'll need a barrow," said a young voice.

Staegrim could have jumped out of his own skin. She was barely nine cycles then, but even so her glare carried so much authority that Staegrim knew he was done for. Her eyes took him in, and the lump in his coat pocket where the stolen golden arm lay, then they moved to the statue standing tall behind him.

"It's too heavy for just one man."

Staegrim blinked. She was in a shift. "Asleep in the day? Do you not go to market?"

The girl shook her head. "I don't like it there, so they leave me here. To watch the house. Good thing too."

"Right." Staegrim looked around for a weapon. Nothing but curtains, paintings, and dark wood. He couldn't just use his hands to end a child now. You had to have some decorum about things.

"There's one in the back."

Staegrim's stomach began to bubble. "One what?"

"A barrow?" said the girl. "So you are as stupid as you look." She *tied her black hair up in a bun. "I'll show you the barrow, but then I'm coming with you."*

"How old are you?" Staegrim barked a laugh. "No, don't tell me. I don't care. And what do you mean coming with me? Coming with me where?"

"Wherever you're going, thief."

Thief? Who did this girl think she was? "My name is Staegrim. Staegrim the Feared. Who are you?"

"Qoreline," said the girl, "but my friends call me Qor. Now do you want that fucking statue or not?"

QOR NEVER DID TELL HIM WHY SHE WANTED AWAY FROM that life, and Staegrim never asked. That little girl looked up at him now, all confused-like, blinking her last blinks, clutching at the sword tip protruding from her stomach, slicing up her hands on the thick steel. There was no ceremony to it, no dramatic grasping at the collar for breath or screams of anguish. Qor just stood there in shock. In denial. Refusing to believe how fragile and weak her body actually was. She was dying like the soldiers she had killed, the men, women, and children whose lives had ended at her hand, yet all Staegrim could think of was how panicked he felt. The unseen swordsman pulled the sword from Qor's back. She fell forward to the ground and Staegrim held his breath as the panic within reached its zenith. In that space where even an eyeblink felt like an age, he waited for the sting of steel, for the cold of mud on his cheek, for the death that—

"You are lucky I value a name, Feared." The Kael stepped over Qor's twitching body. "Words are empty, but names have meaning. And for some reason, Feared, your name struck a chord with me today."

"But why?"

The Kael shrugged. "Why do we do anything? Really?

Nothing has any meaning, so why do we attach meaning to things? It is a search that every being in Rengas takes part in, whether they choose to or not. Your partner's death may indeed have meaning, but you can be damned sure, Feared, that whatever significance you see, is not what I see." He stood up straight. "But that is why I am here. And you are there."

"Someone once told me something very similar."

"Then you were right to have heeded it. You are granted asylum, Staegrim the Feared. Welcome to the lords' army." Staegrim moved aside as the Kael and the guilded swordsman stepped away.

A lump formed in Staegrim's throat. He'd always liked Qor, but there were only two reasons why Rathe would have told them the real count of lords to rebels: they'd be accepted into the lords' ranks or they would be killed. He hadn't thought it could have been both. Seems that two bastards was one too many.

"Kael!" came a panicked shout from outside. "Come quickly!"

The two sides were still fighting as Staegrim took a place at the Kael's side on the hilltop. The Tsiorc had retreated some way back up their hill, and the lords had followed, advancing on the soldiers as they vacated their gained ground.

It was then he saw the plumes of dust blowing out from the valley floor. They burst upwards, grazing the low clouds. The earth groaned, shrieking as the rocky mantle tore and crumbled, tossing masses of fighters aside like matchsticks. Men, women, and Bohr alike fell to their knees as the ground shook, and a great slab of valley floor rose up like a ramp, splitting the armies and leaving only a handful of lords at the bottom of the Tsiorc hill. Great pits of liquid mud opened up, dragging down whole squads of retreating lords struggling and drowning into the ground. The spewing columns of sand subsided as the great slab of valley floor rose over and above the remaining lords' soldiers, hanging for a sickening moment until it broke off like a melting berg, dropping a million tons of earth and rock upon those men. There was no time to shout, scream or pray. It was a spectacular thing to behold, watching an entire army disappear in a heartbeat. His mammy wouldn't have believed it either, to see so many die so quickly, and she was a bad bitch—she'd killed a fair few. Not like this though, thousands of men buried alive all at once.

The Kael just stood there, speechless, a commander with no army to command. Of the three legions, there were perhaps fifty men able to lift themselves free of the avalanche of mud like the dead walking. They stumbled and fell down the sides of it, bumping into stone and rock only to reach the bottom as broken corpses themselves. An eerie silence settled upon the valley. The Forbringrs had spoken.

"PULL BACK," ROARED LAEB, THROWING HIS ARMS TOWARDS the hilltop. "Push harder! Harder! Get up there!"

Never before had he wished to see the faces of the officers and Commander Suilven as much as he wanted to now and never before had this hill seemed so steep.

"Keep going!"

The earthquake had shaken the foundation of the Tsiorc soldiers, but the retreat had blessedly come at the perfect time, keeping almost the entire Tsiorc force out of harm's way. The rising valley floor had obscured everything else, but Laeb was hopeful that the lords' army had at least suffered some losses before the inevitable reengagement.

"Captain! You're alive!" The whites of Kavik's eyes were stark against his muddy face.

Laeb grabbed the offered hand and hauled himself up past

the last few rocks onto the plateau where the officers should have been. "Where've they gone? Where the hell is Suilven?"

Kavik panted for a moment, looking more stressed than exhausted. "Just upped and left. Suilven said something about maintaining a quorum of decision-makers. Reckon they thought the other valleys might meet the same fate as this one. Guess that leaves you in charge, Captain."

The veteran guard Orst appeared out of the throng of bustling, mud-splattered Tsiorc now crowding upon the brow of the hill. "They're gone, Cap! All of 'em. Just gone."

"I know, Orst! But at least the commander is alive, we'll marry up with them when we've pulled the—"

Orst shook his head. "No, Cap. The lords. The Bohr. They're dead. All of 'em."

"They can't be."

"I saw it with my own eyes," said Orst. He took off his helmet and scratched at the greying stubble. "The earth just lifted right up and broke off. Took the whole body of the army together in one fell swoop. Gone. Buried. The lot of 'em. I never saw the likes of it. Not on my daughter's grave." He kissed his fist then held it to his heart. "The Forbringr stands with us this day."

There was barely any time to think on Orst's words before the ground began rumbling anew. Perhaps Suilven had been right to leave when he did.

"It's a tearing aftershock! Orst, get up here—"

The hillside shifted, as slick as water off a shark's back, and Orst flung himself forward, grasping at gauntleted hands, but the ground lurched again, and the guard slid away before Laeb or Kavik could reach him.

"ORST!"

The edge of the plateau where Orst had been standing crumbled, taking the turf with it. Great rocks, buried for a thousand millennia, were set free, rolling downhill and leaving gauges that caved in and dragged the hilltop down the vertical embankment, slamming into the bodies of those who had been too slow to reach the top.

Kavik grabbed Laeb and pulled him back from the edge. "He's gone, Laeb. Come on! We can't stay here!" Kavik hauled Laeb onto the back of a horse, and then they were tearing along the low ridge behind the rest of the Tsiorc rebels.

He looked back at what remained of the battle ground as the ridge climbed higher. Orst had been right, the lord's army had been completely destroyed. A three ton of men, women, and Bohr buried alive under earth and rock. Laeb should have exalted, yet he couldn't find the strength. The gods, the fates, the stars, or whoever had handed them a victory when the battle should have been lost. He should have thanked them, but something deep in his guts wouldn't allow it. If the gods had indeed entered the game, more death would follow.

As survivors raced to safety around him, as the earth drummed with hooves beneath him, he knew one thing only —this was just the beginning.

THE END

Thank you for reading my novella and supporting my work. If I can beg you further to leave a review on Amazon or Goodreads you'll help me reach more people. Even better, if you know someone who likes fantasy give them this book to read. Word of mouth is the best marketing a lowly author like me could ask for.

Read the next part of the story with the first 3 chapters of RINGLANDER: THE PATH AND THE WAY which are included for FREE, beginning on the next page.

mjackson.co.uk | @mikestepjack

CHAPTER 1 - KYIRA

RINGLANDER: THE PATH AND THE WAY

Kyira dragged her belt blade through the slaver's throat, acutely aware of each tendon and muscle tugging on the fine serrated edge. Warm blood burst out over her hand; she had taken the vein. A momentary flutter, but she clenched the bone handle and completed the movement, as though she were simply preparing a pig for the Feast of Moons.

Even as the slaver fell, another emerged from the mist, taller than the last by two heads and twice as wide. His minksin swirled behind him — a wide canvas larger than her sleeping mat. She set her feet as he barrelled towards her, spinning a two-handed ortaxe above his head with one arm. Kyira dove and slid into the plug of ice she had hauled out barely an hour before and sprang back to her feet.

"All he wanted to know was if you had any friends out here, girl," rasped the huge slaver. "The Kin would save you all. Might even let you go if you had a map or two." His deep-set eyes took her in. "I guess not. Still, that ain't no problem of mine. My reckonings tell me that you're out here all by yourself. There ain't no one what can save you."

"Get back!" snarled Kyira, swiping a nervous fish blade out in front.

"I don't think so, girl. Not me. You might be quick enough to catch old Okvik off guard, but not me, little one. Not Siskin."

Kyira shifted left, feigning an escape.

"Oh, no you don't!" The slaver rushed forward, realising too late that the ice hole lay between them. His feet slipped as he tried to fight his own momentum but he slid awkwardly in, coming to a stop with one arm and leg stretching out of the hole. "Curse you!" Guttural pants punctuated each word. "Forbringrs curse you!" His muscles shook as he struggled, searching for purchase on the sharp edges.

Kyira held her belt blade low but steady. The slaver's ortaxe sat just out his reach but it was heavy enough to rebalance him. He clearly had the same thought.

"Raaaa!" He thrust out his arm and clasped the weapon's handle, but the move shifted his weight the wrong way and he slid into the hole like a fat seal. She turned away.

No splash? "Shiach!"

She spun on her spot and peered into the ice hole. The slaver was holding his head a barely a finger's breadth from the slushy surface, the metal point of his ortaxe rammed into the wall, giving him enough tension to hold himself rigid against the inside. He was strong, but those great muscles were shaking, and he was holding his breath. It was silent again, but not the silence when useful things were being done. This was that special quiet that came before death, before the old ox was slaughtered, before the dog that had bitten its master was put down, before the pig...

Kyira side-stepped around the hole, away from the slaver's head and tapped the crook of his knee with her moccasin. The tension broke, his grip failed, and the slushy Laich swallowed him with barely a sound.

She stared at the gently bobbing ice, as though his wide mottled face might somehow emerge, angry and dripping, ready to exact hateful vengeance, but she knew better. His pig heart had beat its last.

She forced her gaze up, scanning the Laich. Mist was not unusual for this time of year, nor this time of day, but it had come on so quickly she had barely finished setting her fishing line when the hills had vanished behind a thick veil. At least she knew exactly where she was, as Pathwatchers always did.

The first slaver was sprawled a few paces away, surrounded by dark spatters. She collected her oil tin but didn't relight it. Slavers always travelled in twos, but there might be more out there yet. She rewound the wick and pressed it into the congealed mixture, then tucked it away in her waist bag.

She squatted over the slaver's corpse, holding her belt blade over his ruined neck. There was no coming back for this pig, but it never hurt to stay cautious. His face was black with Lines but there was no elegance to them, and they had no story to tell — nothing she could make out anyway. She touched her chin, feeling the raised patterns and following them to her cheeks. Each of the five Lines marked her cycles since becoming an adult, the beginning of her story, her aspirations, and her life. A Pathwatcher's life.

She blinked at the slaver. His Lines were those of a fishman, a chaser of sharks, and yet here he was inland, chasing down simple folk. The Sami had a name for those who ignored the Lines written into their skin: Culdè, and this man's aspirations looked as though they had been forgotten many moons ago. Where his skin wasn't Lined, it was cracked and red. A Southerner, not used to the cold, dry winds of Nord, and judging by the beige patches on his breeches, he'd spent weeks, maybe months, in the saddle.

She rummaged through his pockets, ignoring the fleas crawling freely between his inner and outer garments: a dirty pipe made from a wood she had never seen before; some flint; some rolled smokeleaf; a chewstick; and a small pouch. She pulled the drawstrings and let the weight inside tip out onto her palm. There was no mistaking it, even in Nord babies sucked on the varnished wooden bulb to help them sleep. So, he *was* a man. A father. What sort of woman would have bred with you? Certainly no Sami, nor any other Nordun woman that Kyira had met.

A colony of dark specks crowded around a spot of blood on his furry hood, and she stood, feeling nauseous. Regardless of who he was, nobody who let themselves get in such a state lasted long out here, not least those who kept their guard down for so long. He had to have had a camp close by, she thought as she dragged him to the ice hole. The body slid along the edge, tipping in headfirst, just like his friend.

The ice plug came next, and it dropped neatly back into the hole, forcing a little water to gurgle up the sides. Pocketing the slaver's pouch, she dipped her hands in the water and scrubbed the blood from her skin, trying to picture which sort of fire would warm her up the quickest. It was a half day's walk from here on the Laich back to where Aki, her father, had camped and she would need to find somewhere along the way to sleep. There were a number of places: the cave upon the fourth sister above the Waning Crescent; a hidden alcove in the small waterfall a league beyond on the last sister — she might get wet, but at least she would be hidden. The cave would be best, and the fourth sister was a tall enough hill to spot anyone following.

The dark residue, colourless in the evening light, pooled with the quickly freezing water creating patterns.

She had not planned on being away from home for so long, but the new season's taimen living in the Laich were far too fat to just leave to the orca, and twilight was the best time to catch them. It was why she had spent most of the day cutting such a big hole through the ice. It was lucky it was not yet spring — things might have gone very differently if she had been fishing for eels.

A noise blew in from the north bank and her breath caught. A whicker. She stared into the darkening night, but the mist gave nothing away.

The belt blade slipped back into a sheath at her waist with a reassuring rasp, its bone handle still sticky with the slaver's blood; the rack of four taimens went over her back, the clasp hooking through the loop on her shoulder; and lastly, her fishing line, which she spun quickly around the gnarlnut shell, was thrust into her waist bag.

It was time to go.

She spared the mist a final glance and sped off over the ice towards the far bank. The frozen estuary was narrow, but she was closer to the northern side than the south. Hard ice crunched underfoot so loud she was sure someone would hear, but she pushed on, reaching the south bank's shoreline well within an hour. She slowed as she approached the rocky outcrops — if there were more slavers, they couldn't have guessed she could cross the Laich so quickly. In any case they were mounted and she was not.

Weaving deftly between the rocks, she leapt over the thinnest ice and onto the shore. The ground was permafrost all year round here along the Taegr — the line that marked the upper circle of the world — and was perfect for running. Only her brother Hasaan could match her stride, but not for long, a fact she used to enjoy teasing him with. The ground was a smear of colour beneath her as her feet carried her on, bounding lightly over and up the fat waist of the second sister, upon and around the ridge of the hill's back and onto the shoulder, the first of the two peaks.

Hopping over a decoy fork, Kyira carried on through into the rough grass until the slightest change of colour showed she had re-joined the ridge path. It was as clear to her as if it had been lain out with lines of oil and set alight. She stopped and turned back towards the Laich.

Three mounted slavers stood at the northern shore, black scratches on the pristine white of the Laich. Kyira ducked. They might not be Nordun but the horned nara they rode upon were, and they would catch her up and run her down before three hours had passed.

She took off, sprinting along the nape — it was slower but the rough ground would hide her shape. The line led her all the way to the shoulders of the third sister, a ridge that led to the highest hill on the Waning Crescent. She trudged carelessly through a large patch of snow as though she was heading down into the valley. Her pursuers would expect her to seek shelter in the vale before risking the ridges on a moonless night.

She raced along the ridge, trying to cover as much distance as she could before first dark. Panting, she dropped off the Waning Crescent and entered the second valley, a tree valley, named not for the trees, of which there were none, but for the multiple ways in and out. It was filled with glacial boulders and was a perfect place to rest and escape if she needed to.

She jumped down the few feet onto the first boulder and ran its length. Ten paces exactly. The next one, six, she thought, already in the air. She landed and rolled forward then again she was air-bound, springing over the stones with ease. The last rock was flat and although she couldn't see it, she knew it was five paces narrow and twenty-and-one-half paces long, with a short step to the grass. She hopped onto it, then jerked as her foot bumped into something that should not have been there, sending her spinning into the sharp edge of a split boulder. The ground barely had time to greet her before she was back up, staring at the dark lump. It was a grey glacial boulder ten paces wide and fifteen long, deposited many moons ago, and had lived at the bottom of this valley since then. Yet here it was, uphill.

"What are you doing up here?" she said, feeling along its edge. "You did not walk, and neither were you pushed. You are too fat for that." It had been split right down the middle. The ragged edge led to a face that was almost shiny, like the rock had spent a lifetime against a smith's forge. What force could split a rock in two?

Irrational panic bubbled in her breast, her heart pounded as though the slavers had somehow appeared before her. She drew a ragged breath, willing the shapes around her back into their still, stoic forms. She was alone.

Breathe.

Her skin tingled and her vision narrowed. The vale grew darker, but somehow clearer as a new focus settled upon her.

Breathe.

Her mother used to call it magic, but it was no such thing. It was just a way of tricking her body into listening. And feeling.

Breathe.

A sympathy with the world, from the crisp air to the frost at her feet.

Breathe.

A snowcrick chirruped on her right, looking for a male to fight. Another to the left. There must be a new nest nearby. She listened as they spoke to each other, imagining that she could understand their noises.

Breathe.

A soft wind bristled at the hairs on her face bringing a new smell.

Wood smoke. There was a fire close by. The vale was almost completely black now, but there... there was something...

Someone was breathing, and it was heavy and laboured. Kyira crept around the split boulder, and pursing her lips, whistled three short bursts, warbling the sound. There was a slight pause before the corresponding call floated in on the breeze.

The dim glow of the fire appeared from between the boulders, flickering shadows coming from the low wall of snow and rocks. A fire built in haste. Kyira stayed just outside of the light.

"Hasaan?" said a man.

"It's me, Aki." She manoeuvred into the hollow depression, skirted the fire, and knelt at her father's side. This was a well-chosen camp; they were well hidden here. "What happened? Why are you out here? It is not safe."

"You think I cannot handle myself?" asked her father, throwing his climbing stick clattering against the stones.

She reached over and moved the stick's leather wrapping away from the coals. "There are dangers. Aki, your skin is so pale."

He drew back. "Child, I am perfectly able—"

"Aki," said Kyira, pulling the taimen from her back and sitting them on the grass.

"Aki, Aki, Aki! Iqaluk is my name, Kyira! Aki is a name children use. You are Lined now. Act like it." He nodded back up the hill. "Where is your brother?"

"He is not with you?"

"He goes his own way. He always has." Even insensible, the words were meant to cut her. "He will be fine. He went climbing this morning."

"So, you are fighting again."

"That boy has much to learn!" snapped Iqaluk, grabbing the stick and shaking it at her. "As do you." He smoothed down his long grey beard.

"And what have I to learn exactly?"

"How to choose your own path for one!"

"I do that which makes me happy, Aki." Sickness rose in Kyira's stomach. "Besides, I know a Stormwing's call when I hear one." It was probably the most lame rebuke she could have chosen, but it was hardly the time to get into a debate on the course of her life.

"Even a Culdè knows the Stormwing, not least during mating season."

"A Culdè? You think I do not know myself!" Kyira spoke before she could stop herself. "Well, I knew you were here, hiding, in this... hole. What if that stone rolled back down? What would you do then by yourself."

"Did you see it? No? I did. It is broken in two, girl! Cracked like an egg, as though there were nothing inside but... but yolk." The last word vanished into a bout of ragged coughs.

Kyira placed a tender hand on his forehead. Fever blood. Only the beginnings, but it would get worse. "Where are you hurt?"

Iqaluk tried to bend forward then after a second patted his thick skin jacket near his kidneys. Carefully, Kyira spread the coat, smelling the blood before she saw it. Her cold hands touched searing hot skin drawing a hiss between clenched teeth. She had never known her father to show pain. He was the strongest man she knew. She lifted his coat and shirt revealing angry red skin surrounding a puncture wound. She pulled the fishing line from her bag and knotted it around the jacket at his back to keep the wound exposed. "Don't move, Aki. I'll be back."

The low bushes and plants hid their medicines well this far north. Thorns and poisons kept all but the most determined animals at bay, but Kyira knew what to look for. Under the last rock and a few inches under the earth was a bulbous, woody weed: a type of inedible tuber root with soft red fur that was smooth one way but not the other. It was smaller than she would've liked but it would do. Heedless of the mud, she dug her hands beneath and gathered up a few wriggling grubs, before stuffing them in the pouch she'd taken from the slaver.

Back at the fire she peeled away the outer layers of the tuber, and sliced along the root's length with her blade, careful not to touch the wet flesh. She waited until its distinctive smell permeated the air and then thrust it into a pile of snow. After a few minutes of preparation, the cold root and the grubs were infusing over the coals in her father's kettle.

Save the sound of bubbling liquid and crackling fire, a familiar silence hung in the air. It was the same quiet that usually followed their family meal, as they sat around tending to skins or sharpening knives, a time where no one spoke, and all felt at peace as their hands worked. Before she died, her mother would wind twine from sheep sinew, expertly weaving thin strands together, plaiting it over and over until it was tight and strong. Her deft fingers always moved so quickly.

Kyira wafted the sickly-sweet kettle steam then plucked out the red root with her knife and dropped it into the coals.

"Aki?" Iqaluk didn't move. "Aki?" He mumbled something. The fever blood was getting worse. "Iqaluk." His eyes opened at his name. "Iqaluk," she said, grabbing his head. "You must drink this." He sipped slowly, spilling some of the hot liquid over himself. By the time he finished he had only regained a little colour.

"Who did this to you?" She felt a fool for asking, seeing as she already knew the answer, but she had to keep him talking.

Iqaluk lay back, breathing deeply. "Slavers," he said, his voice high. "They were mounted."

"What did they want? What did they take?"

"Everything, child. Everything. They raided our supplies.

The animals are all dead and burned. We have nothing left, Kyira. Nothing."

"We will rebuild. We have done it before, Aki, and we shall do it again."

His hard stare softened. "Your words fill me with hope, but sometimes words can be as meaningless as the canvas upon which they are printed. You have to drive change and forge your path!"

Kyira nodded but couldn't stop herself taking a long breath. He had been talking like this more and more of late, imparting wisdom as though he might die in the night.

"Not every fight needs to be fought, Aki."

"I will not let these men get away with this! We will only find ourselves fighting more of them come spring. Let us kill this one at the seed." He propped himself up on a wobbling elbow. "Where is Vlada?"

Kyira worked her fingers. "I don't know. I sent him up to hunt, just before they came."

Iqaluk sat up. "Before who came?" Drops of sweat had appeared on his brow and beside his nose — the medicine was working.

"I was attacked."

Iqaluk's eyes widened, and he tried to get up. "By who?"

"No, please, Aki. Please. I am fine. I dealt with it."

"Good. Slavers care only for coin. They would sooner sneak into our camp in the dead of night and raid us in our sleep, only so they can attack the next day with the odds in their favour. That is if they didn't slit your throat while you dreamt. They are fools and cowards."

"They wanted maps."

"Maps," snorted Iqaluk, reeling like a drunkard. "Kyira, when the breathe of the Forbringrs carved the first paths, it was the ways of the Kartta, the first of our people, that shaped the world."

He wasn't talking sense. "Shaped the world? Aki, please."

"Listen to me, Kyira! It is up to *us* to shape the world. The practice of documenting the paths was abandoned centuries ago, we must pass it down... as treasure to the next... next generation." He winced and his eyes rolled. "Even the slavers know... would know this."

"Aki, you must sleep."

"Yes, you are right. I will need my energy if I am to climb Hasaan's peak tonight."

Kyira's mouth opened in protest but was stilled as her father's hand rose to her cheek following the Lines on her skin.

"My daughter. You are as fierce as your mother ever was, and more. You will make a fine Pathwatcher. If only your brother were... if only... if..." He closed his eyes, and his chest began rising and falling with the heavy rhythm of sleep.

CHAPTER 2 - ALL FOR SHOW
RINGLANDER: THE PATH AND THE WAY

The sun dropped behind the distant hills, casting the black and green plains on each side of the wagons into soft purples and reds. Even the odd gnarled tree poked out of the ground — an uncommon sight in Nord — its bark as black as scorched earth with fingers that reached upwards at the twilight sky. The plains gave way to high cliffs that rose up like city walls in the distance just begging to be climbed. Hasaan swallowed the lump in his throat as he realised this was the last time he would ever see them. Iqaluk would still climb them of course, but even he preferred to stay amongst the hilltops, it seemed that the flatter lands just enraged his fool of a father. Kyira was more calm at least, but still a bloody awful climber. He was sure she'd rather run for miles around the cliff face than attempt to climb it. He would have beaten her either way.

The trailer of the wagon had sweated pitch all over him, hands, tan boots and all, making the bumpy ride along the old road even less comfortable. The dense layers of his minksin offered plenty of protection against the cold, but not from ill-fitting slats nor rusted rivets digging into his rear. Besides, with all the other conscripts there was barely room for him to sit, let alone be comfortable, so he endured it quietly.

Cailaen sat crumpled next to him, head lolling back and forth while a line of drool snaked its way across his cheek. Cailaen was his brother, not by blood but by experience. No one had come close to being there for him as Cailaen had, whether it was seeing off the Dearg twins at the Nortun settlement when they were barely babes or being offered a hand at the right time on a challenging climb. They never spoke of the link, but it was there, and they both knew it. Cailaen snored and Hasaan rolled his eyes, looking straight up into the grimy face of a young girl across from him. She eyed him up and down openly through a flash of blonde hair hanging over her right eye. The rest of her hair was dyed black, which placed her from one of the Uigur clans, perhaps even the same clan Hasaan's mother had come from. He stared back, wondering if he would have to fight her. Maybe he might even have to kill her before they arrived in the capital city. He could do it. The damned earth, he would do it, if he had to. Iqaluk would disapprove of even just thinking such a thing, but then he disapproved of everything. The old man knew nothing about who Hasaan really was. Nobody did. He was vicious, powerful and perfectly capable of killing. If he had to.

The wagon crunched to a stop, and both lines of conscripts slid towards the front in a heap.

"Out!" cried the rider, swinging down from the nara pulling their wagon. The creature hissed and threw its sprawling antlers towards him. "Ya!" He fumbled at his side, and the animal quieted as a long leather whip unravelled to the road. "Yeah, you better flinch, if you know what's good for you!" He turned back to the conscripts and bared a gummy set of yellow teeth. "You lot, out!"

Each wagon in the caravan slowly emptied as their riders

swore and shouted and threatened and whipped. They were all adorned in shimmering leathery skins from an animal Hasaan didn't know and while most of them had scars upon their faces only their rider had Lines. They were more crude than his own, colouring everything from nose to neck in black patchy ink. The rider caught his eye and pulled aside his iridescent coat to reveal a curved sword as long as his leg. "Git out!"

"It's all for show, Hassi," yawned Cailaen.

"I know," lied Hasaan. "By the way, thanks for leaving me alone with this lot."

Cailaen smirked. "Friend, I can talk small with the best of them. You, on the other hand, could do with the practice."

A whip cracked above their heads, and they both jumped up jostling with the rest out of the wagon into an untidy line.

"I swear," growled Hasaan, "if that thing hits me it'll be the last thing he ever does." He pushed at the boy in front. "Hurry up!" The boy turned and sneered as he stepped down off the trailer. "I don't remember being such a shit when I was that age." He added a sneer of his own and the boy turned away and dropped down from the wagon.

"Maybe they're a bit sore from being drafted into an army?" said Cailaen, dryly. "Wrong place, wrong time," said Hasaan.

They both jumped down and Cailaen tapped Hasaan on the chest proudly. "Or right place, right time."

The rider swished and flicked the sword as the conscripts formed a rough line. He looked capable with it, but Hasaan got the impression those flourishes wouldn't help in a real sword fight. He shared a glance with Cailaen. All for show.

Conscripts from other wagons were already scuttling back and forth with boxes, blankets and saddles by the time their rider finally lowered his sword.

"For those that joined us in, whatever that last settlement

was," he announced, "I am Gorm, First to Commander Lor." He paused to let the mighty words sink in. "We will be camping here this night, whereupon the commander himself will be joining us." He pushed his hand in between Hasaan and the Uigur girl making a show of separating the line into two. "In the meantime, you lot will set up canvas, and believe me when I say I want all groundsheets lashed tightly, because if I wake up one more morning on stingmoss I'll feed you to the fuckin nara!"

"Do they even eat meat?" whispered Cailaen.

Hasaan gave a snort. In truth he didn't know, but they were bigger than horses and those antlers were as thick as his arm. "We do. Maybe we should cut one down and cook it!"

"Yeah," said Cailaen. "Best I do it, though. Not sure you're ever going to be much use with a sword."

"Swords are only useful close up," said Hasaan, tapping the wrapping strapped to his back. "I prefer to keep my enemies at a distance."

Gorm moved the front of the line along, slapping the flat of his sword against any exposed skin that strayed too close. "That's right, off you go. And you lot..." he said, turning back to Hasaan and Cailaen's group. "The first to catch at least twelve squirrels eats tonight. I know when the other two riders get back they will be hungry. Now go." Cailaen rolled his eyes but set off with the remaining six conscripts towards the plain behind them. "Bear in mind I'll be taking half of them for myself," shouted Gorm after them.

"Can you not hunt for yourself?"

"What was that?"

Hasaan picked up a small round pebble the size of his thumb. "I said, can you not hunt for yourself?" He tossed the stone in the air and caught it. "I can catch a squirrel, any time of the day or night, even with this little stone, that is how good I am at hunting. But I would never ask someone else to

MICHAEL S. JACKSON

catch one for me, let alone twelve." He stepped towards Gorm. "Then, I must assume that you cannot hunt."

Gorm moved to lift the sword, but it was too long and the space between them too short. "So, you're the one. The one with illusions of grandness. A Sami boy with barely three cycles since his Lines were drawn on by his mother."

Hasaan shook his head to hear such badly pronounced Nordun. This fool was a Southerner make no mistake. "Seven."

"What?"

"It has been seven cycles since my name day."

Gorm stepped back and pointed the sword at Hasaan's chest. "Really, now. You're younger than you look then. What's your name?"

Hasaan stretched to his full height. "Hasaan."

"And why are you here?"

"To fight."

"*You* have come to fight with the lord's army, and for the Bohr? What do you think you can offer the Bohr king?"

"My service."

"In that case, I suggest you listen to me. I have the ear of the commander, and I can tell you he does not take kindly to slackness," he pointed to a long scar behind his ear, "or candour. Unless you want to walk all the way to Tyr." The tip of his sword trailed down Hasaan's minksin and stopped at his feet. "Or at least as long as your legs hold out, then you'll be dragged until there is nothing left but a red smear." His sneer twisted into an ugly smile. "But we all deserve one infraction. A chance to learn and be taught. So, while I muse upon what I am to do with you why don't you catch us all something tasty and fat. Go on now. Fuck off."

IT WAS THE MIDDLE OF NIGHT AND STILL THE CONSCRIPTS rushed between orders, carrying packages, grooming nara, and prepping the animals for another day of solid walking. Other, more fortunate conscripts were sparring between themselves, using short swords and small knives under the watchful stare of one or two riders.

Hasaan took a pebble from a large pile and pressed it into the soggy earth next to two others. "And that's three," he said, with a sigh. "Do they really have to be in threes?"

A lanky conscript called Ander looked up and nodded. "Groups of three is what he said. Perfect groups of three."

"The death of me, Hassi," hissed Cailaen, from his left. "The death of me."

Ander leant in towards them both. "This ain't the half of it. Night before last he had two of the other lot searching for scrabs all night."

"Scrabs?" said Hasaan.

"Without lamps," added Ander.

Cailaen turned towards Hasaan. "An entire night chasing beetles."

Hasaan ignored them and pressed another stone into the mud, trying not to think about the rumbling in his guts. He and Cailaen had eaten well before joining in Nortun, but that was well over a day ago, and while the smell of charred squirrel meat had long since left the air, his stomach remembered it vividly.

"An entire night," hissed Cailaen, thumping Hasaan's arm.

Ander leaned in again. "I heard two escaped earlier today."

Hasaan frowned. "Escaped? From what?"

Ander shrugged. "Not all joined willingly. You saw the lines of them in Makril—"

"Quiet!" spat Keene. "The lot of you! You want that idiot rider to come down again?"

Hasaan spared the girl a contemptuous look. Her face was even grimier now, but in the high moonlight she looked not too bad. Even pretty.

Cailaen caught his eye. "Nice, isn't she?" he whispered, eyebrows dancing.

"Mmm. You think she's an Uigur?"

"Could be," whispered Cailaen.

Hasaan stole another glance. Those who could shoot had a certain way about the way they moved. "They're said to be near unstoppable with a bow in the hand."

"Maybe she's Sami."

"She's not Sami."

"Why, because she knows how to rub pitch in her hair?" Cailaen's breath blew in over his ear. "She likes girls."

"What! How do you know?"

"Just a hunch," said Cailaen, making a spectacle of placing his stone just right. "I've seen her leering over them almost as much as you." Hasaan scrabbled the dirt around Cailaen's stones. "Oh no. Now, I'll have to begin again."

Hasaan's laugh blurted out before he could stop it, and Gorm's rickety form appeared over them. "I have some barrels needing broken down," he said. "And then put back together. Only after the stones have all been half-buried." He turned to walk away, then stopped and turned back. "And then dug back up." His laughter followed him until he was out of sight.

Keene stared at Hasaan. "You two will get us all kicked out before we've come close to being Earned! Either that or just hang us, and I'm far from being done!" She resumed burying the pebbles piled up beside her, punching them into the ground.

Hasaan sighed. Was this the reward for joining the lord's army? Eight hours a day performing menial tasks that served no purpose?

"You should probably at least pretend to care," said Cailaen, interrupting Hasaan's thoughts. "Seeing as you put us here."

"I've never known you to care about anything, Cailaen. What makes this life so different?"

"Keene is right. Once we're Earned everything changes. We'll be story makers of kings. Trust me!"

"Story makers?"

"We'll have whole squadrons of men under us who we can command. Men twice our age!"

"How?"

Cailaen looked bewildered. "Because we're First!"

Hasaan stared blankly at him.

"Come on, Hassi. Do you not listen to anything I say? The first of our bloodline. The first of any bloodline to serve in the lord's army are almost guaranteed to become Earned. You remember Nevin? He left Nord after the Dearg twins jumped him one time too many. Story says he was one of the Kin and now he's Earned. Our age, and he's Earned! He's in charge of a squadron of nine men."

Hasaan could picture it: gleaming armour, a home in the most prosperous city in the world, a wife, children, fame and fortune. "I won't be able to climb in a city."

Cailaen's pressed his lips together. "You said to me not two days ago, that it doesn't matter where we end up. That this is a way out. Sure, my father might not be breathing down my neck as hard as yours, but I still have the exact same expectations on my shoulders. So, don't give me a story of how oppressed you are. We're all running from something."

Hasaan nodded at Keene. "Even her?"

"Maybe not her. I think she's here to make everyone's life difficult. But Ander is hiding from his two uncles. They want him to be a goat farmer."

"He does look like a goat farmer."

Cailaen nodded. "Exactly! You see what I'm saying, brother. We're the oldest here by at least two cycles."

Hasaan considered interrupting but settled for a loud sigh instead.

"Brother, we can own these people. All we have to do is stay the course. We are special. Unless you would prefer to just do what your father wants."

Hasaan shook his head slowly. "Watching paths."

"Maintaining a set of muddy trails through the wilderness. For the rest of your life."

"But this is all just so... pointless." Hasaan looked back at his friend, then down at the small round pebble in his palm. He threw it over Keene's head into a stagnant pool behind her drawing sharp looks from her mucky face.

"She'll take your head off, Hassi! Don't push her."

"So, it's not just pitch in her hair then," said Hasaan, smiling. "Cail. Come on, fight me."

"What?"

"Fight me. Like we used to. Properly though or they won't believe it. I'm fed up and anything is better than this. Let's show them what we're made of." Hasaan brought the heel of his boot into the neat lines of pebbles in front of Cailaen, and dragged it back tearing out a long divot of turf. "Come on."

"After what I just said, you want to start a fight?"

Hasaan open handed Cailaen across the face, catching him perfectly. He rubbed his stinging fingertips. "Now?"

Cailaen's expression didn't change. His ability to take a punch was one of the things Hasaan loved about him. The Dearg twins couldn't touch the two of them, not with his quick hands and Cailaen's apparently dead nerves.

He flexed his hand and moved in for another but Cailaen sprung up right into Hasaan's guts and they both fell to the mud in a heap. A second later and they were circling each other, ignoring the protests of Ander and Keene as they trampled through their neat lines of stones.

Cailaen feigned right then switched left in an effort to unbalance him, the same move he always pulled, and as Hasaan threw his weight sideways, he left a leg out. Cailaen clipped it and ploughed into the other conscripts.

He pushed himself up, pulling bits of ground from his teeth. "That was a dirty move."

"Yeah well maybe you should—" Keene's hook caught Hasaan in the jaw, sending him to the dirt. It took a moment for the light to return fully, and when it did, he turned to see Ander swinging wildly at her. Cailaen sat grinning across from Hasaan, trying to stay out of the way. Then their eyes locked and they were back up and wrestling again. Cailaen was smaller but somehow still managed to grab Hasaan in a headlock, while behind them Keene was expertly jabbing someone who looked as though they had only been standing watching. Hasaan laughed, and grabbed Cailaen from behind, pulling him up at the waist and squeezing as tightly as he could.

"Argh!" shouted Cailaen, as Hasaan lifted him clear above his head.

"Haha!" roared Hasaan, but his elbow buckled and both of them tumbled to the wet earth. Hasaan dragged himself back up. "Again!" But Cailaen was staring back up at the road, along with Keene, Ander and the rest of them.

A pale nara trotted along the narrow road, expertly manoeuvring around the many potholes, and guided by a huge man; the biggest Hasaan had ever seen. A girl stumbled alongside, hands tied to the stirrup of the rider's saddle. The nara turned revealing a young man tied in the same way on the other side. They looked dishevelled and dirty as though they had been dragged along the ground. The nara stopped and a huddle of conscripts gathered around them.

"Come on," whispered Cailaen, clambering up the bank.

"I think he's the commander," whispered Hasaan, as they reached the back of the huddle. "He's huge."

"He's Bohr."

The rider was seven feet tall and bald but for a long topknot that sprouted from the middle of his head and disappeared behind him. His jacket was stiff and grey, and flashed with red around the collar and cuffs while an aura of danger surrounded him likes waves of heat. Gorm walked over to meet the pale mount and held the nara's reins as the Commander swung smoothly down. His cold stare raked over each of them, and Hasaan felt his insides go cold.

"You are no one," said the commander in accented Sami, his voice like gravel in a tin. "Singularly you have no purpose. Only together do you exist now, and for those that make it, you will be one of thousands who will fight with you and for you. You will provide a necessary arm to the Bohr armies, providing resource and resupply to those in battle. You may even be chosen to fight in the lord's army." He scanned the circle. "Although only a few will ever see the inside of the barracks at Tyr."

"Resource and resupply?" hissed Hasaan, sideways at Cailaen. "I thought you said we were here to fight?"

Cailaen winked. "We'll beat them all, Hassi. The story makers of kings..." He nodded forward.

A hush had drawn over the conscripts. Gorm was freeing the boy and girl from the saddle.

"Until that time," continued the Commander, "you will have to prove that you belong. If you feel that this life is not for you then Gorm here will find other uses for you. His word is final."

Gorm pulled the boy and girl away from the nara and stood them to face the line of conscripts.

Hasaan's breath caught. They were brother and sister, except he had not seen them since they had left the town of

Makril. They were young, and both had the same brown hair and bright eyes as the man who had offered them up for service.

Gorm lifted the girl's chin and moved close enough to kiss her.

She stared back defiantly, but her chin was wobbling.

"Deserter!" he shouted, spraying the girls face with spit.

Something about her reminded Hasaan of his sister, either the way she stood, or the way she held herself. Would Kyira have let herself be caught and corralled like an escaped goat? There was a scuffle of feet on earth and Gorm's fist crashed into her face breaking her nose. She crumpled to the ground, and the brother moved to intervene, but Gorm knocked him down with a heavy shoulder. The boy struggled up and Gorm smiled. Another punch, but this time the boy took it. Again, and again, and again, Gorm pummelled him until the sister clawed at Gorm's legs, pleading and crying and squealing, but her brother stayed standing, his face a bloodied pulp around red eyes that could surely barely see. Hot bile rose in Hasaan's throat as Gorm unsheathed that long sword from within his coat and paced back and forth spinning the blade in the space between the prisoners and the conscripts. The commander watched on silently, with no emotion.

Hasaan should have looked away — it was clear what was coming — but something held his gaze. His choices had led him here, and he would honour them, and hold to them because what else did you have but the choices you make?

"Pleash!" mumbled the sister, hauling herself up and standing in front of her brother. "Leave him!"

Hasaan's resolve broke. His heart hammered. His foot twitched. He had to do something, honour or no.

Cailaen's hand grabbed at his wrist. "Hassi. No. Don't."

Gorm taunted the deserters, pretending to cry and pout. Mocking them like the Dearg twins used to mock Cailaen.

Hasaan had stopped them once that day he and Cailaen had become friends and brothers, and maybe he could stop this. He had to do something. He had to.

"What did they do?!"

"Deserters," snapped the commander.

Gorm nodded. "Ran away night before last, so they did. Now they got to pay the price."

Gorm turned to face the girl, and she spat blood into his face. He spun the sword, and cracked the hilt into the bridge of her broken nose. A killing blow. Stunned, her body held rigid, then she fell motionless to the rider's feet.

The brother dropped to his knees, feeling at her broken face while his own bled over her. "Rian! Rian!"

Gorm took the boy by the arm and lifted him to standing. "Come on," He didn't resist as Gorm led him to the middle of the circle, turning him just so to face Hasaan.

The boy just stood there as Gorm planted his feet. Hasaan wanted to cry out, but it was too late. The boy jerked as the sword pushed through, the tip of it flashing briefly through his chest. He staggered backwards as Gorm pulled the sword free, then fell upon the body of his sister.

Confusion washed over Hasaan, followed quickly by deep dread. He was aware of his body, but he couldn't feel anything. The world beyond that boy and girl didn't exist. It was only when the commander stepped forward that Hasaan realised that he had stepped out of line.

The Bohr's words were now only for him. "There will be stops along the way," he said, stepping over the deserter's bodies, "and some of you will be asked to do questionable things. If you disregard anything that I or any other rider asks of you, your life is forfeit. If you leave, your life is forfeit. If you turn upon your own, your life is forfeit." The words were a sword, held to Hasaan's chest, directed at him and him alone. "You belong to the lord's army. You are the Kin."

CHAPTER 3 - THE GODS THEMSELVES

RINGLANDER: THE PATH AND THE WAY

The tuber root was medicinal, but along with its fixing properties it sometimes created visions if left to stew. Nordun peddlers harvested the root for exactly that reason, drying and pounding it into powder to extend its life. They called it Tomha and used it to treat wounds and long nights alike. Kyira had never found a reason for carrying Tomha powder with her; there was always a fresh root to be had somewhere. She had removed the root from the kettle, well before it should have got to the stage where it caused visions, and yet her father was pulling himself up the cliff face as though he was a young man again. He was as high as a bird, and in more ways than one. The concoction had knocked him out for near half an hour, after which he had awoken and immediately insisted they find Hasaan. They had arrived shortly after at Hammer, one of the highest peaks around Nortun and indeed Nord itself — Hasaan's favourite climb.

"Ho!"

Kyira had just enough time to bring her hands over her face as Iqaluk's stepping rope whipped down in front of her.

She reached out, feeling the fibres beneath her fingertips then squinted down into the darkness. An icy blast of wind slapped at her face, passing through her thick skin jacket like it was not there. There was no sign that they had already climbed half the mountain. They could have been but a few metres from the ground were it not for the misery gradually filling her stomach like rising tsampa bread. On top of everything, Vlada's absence gnawed at her. She longed for the feel of his weight upon her arm, and his powerful claws pinching her skin. Her fool brother would be fine, he always was. Hasaan would often disappear only to return a day or a week later. He was as stubborn as their father, which was most of their problem. Vlada, however, hadn't stayed away this long since first learning to fly, not that he would mind the freedom — he was probably gorging himself on deer or ox at this very moment. She inhaled and pursed her lips, catching the whistle before the sound blew out of her cheeks. No. She couldn't call him. Not when enemies might be nearby.

Breathe.

She jumped for the first knot, feeling a split second of panic as her weight fell and brought the knot in tight. The rope whipped out sideways, dangling her precariously over the sheer face.

"Open your eyes, child!" roared Iqaluk, over the wind.

"They are open, you fool!"

"Accept that you are in danger and open your eyes!"

Breathe.

Her over-zealous jump had taken her completely past the first knot and onto the second. The rope kicked out again, but this time she countered the movements, forcing her upper body as straight as she could, leaving her feet to hang loose, and slowing the rope to a gentle swing.

She squeezed the thin rope tightly between her thighs and shuffled up one knot at a time, shoving her foot into any part of the rock that would take it. The cliff face stretched up and over her head in a long overhang that looked like the head of a huge hammer bursting out from the side of the hillside, with her rope anchored off to the right of it. Why hadn't they just gone around?

"Aki! Where are you?"

"Ho!" came his voice, closer than she expected. His head appeared over the edge of a hidden alcove, imperceptible from the surrounding rock.

"Aki, I'm... it's too high. Help me!"

There was no reply.

She growled at the man's thick-headedness. Imagine bringing her up here in the first place. What a fool he was! She planted both feet on the rock to steady herself and walked up over the edge. "Why didn't you help me!" she shouted. "Are you hearing me? I almost fell!"

A red trail glistened on the pale lichen leading to her father where he sat. He said nothing, and just stared back out over the valley. "Even the Forbringrs could not have brewed such."

Illuminated from within by some unnatural light, a huge spherical cloud hung above a hill in the distance — the first sister of the Waning Crescent. The bruised sky jerked and pulsed like a heart still beating as it consumed the mist from the surrounding vales, drawing it up the hillsides like lifeblood in thick lines. The air was charged, electric like before a lightforks storm but within that cloud the forks held fast — the pulsing veins of the Gods themselves.

"I've heard tales of such things before," said Iqaluk, not taking his eyes from it. "Clouds that spin so quickly as to suck up everything in their path, consuming entire cities within a heartbeat."

Kyira couldn't speak. The immensity of it shocked her. It was so big it could crush these hills flat.

"We need to find shelter," said Iqaluk.

The top of the Hammer was only a short climb away beyond their position, and the summit mostly flat, covered in grass and lichen. By the time they'd reached it, the cloud had flattened into a huge disc that stretched out towards them, its wispy fingers grasping and quivering at the centre of the disc, but with no more mist to consume leaving the drop down the Hammer's sheer face unnervingly present. The low cloud around the Waning Crescent began to shudder, gathering until all at once the whole sky itself dropped around them. Kyira fell to her knees, hands above her head as though she might somehow prop it up. She shouted, but her words were snatched by the whirling clouds around her. She couldn't move. Her frozen limbs were locked to the ground as though she were a metal plate stuck to a lodestone. A strange buzzing reverberated through her from the hill below, and suddenly she was part of the hillside. She was not Kyira of the Sami people, nor the daughter of Iqaluk and Thea, sister to Hasaan or master to Vlada, she was the land, the earth, a speck of life that could be rubbed out on the whim of the Gods.

A brilliant floating point of blue fire, bright against the clear night sky, hung above the eye of the storm now nestled in the valley below. Lightforks licked up to it from the spinning whirlwind, surrounding it in a net of crackling light and drawing it down. As soon as it touched the hillside, it shrank into itself and grew so bright that the stars above vanished.

"Get down!" Iqaluk threw himself over her, but it did nothing to stop it.

Eyes screwed shut, Kyira held her ears and screamed as some force threw her against damp earth. Rocks bit into her side; dirt scraped her cheek. A shadow loomed above, and she was dragged upwards. The earth beneath had torn itself up and was sliding back towards the Hammer's overhang, with Kyira along with it, riding it like a sled. She scrambled for something to hold, snatching at the rope just out of reach, at the earth, at the air. The slab of earth teetered on the edge, snagging on the rocks, then rose upwards into the air away from the Hammer's summit, as some unknown force tore it away from the mountainside. Iqaluk's stick hovered in front and Kyira grabbed hold of it and as the earth slab lifted off the side of the mountain. The stick held firm, dragging her sideways to tumble back into the pit left by the missing earth.

Kyira looked up perplexed as more slabs of earth floated over them and the summit like raevens gliding on the wind.

"Daughter! Are you alright?"

Kyira sat up and threw her arms around him. "Aki!"

Iqaluk embraced her then pulled her away. "Look."

The sky was full of debris torn from the hilltops and pulled towards the Waning Crescent's peaks. Kyira and Iqaluk stood watching until the slabs slowed, then stopped a thousand paces above the vale, just hanging in the air. Then they fell. It was like a wave, the closest to the Waning Crescent falling first. One slab blew Kyira's braids back as it hurtled towards the earth along the sheer face. It smashed onto the great boulders below along with the sound of a hundred wet thwumps that echoed around the hills.

When the last echo had all but vanished, Kyira turned back to the Waning Crescent. The hillside around the first sister had fallen away completely, leaving a quarry of mud that stretched back to the valley floor. A needle spire of rock, too thin to be so tall stood above it all higher than the peak.

"Where did that come from?"

"I don't know," uttered Iqaluk, "whatever caused the Gods to be so angry." He turned toward her, eyes wide. "But we have to find Hasaan. We need to find him, at all cost."

Thank you for reading the first 3 chapters of THE PATH AND THE WAY, Book 1 in the RINGLANDER SERIES.

eBook available from Amazon.
Physical copies available online from all good book stores.

mjackson.co.uk | @mikestepjack

RINGLANDER
Book 1

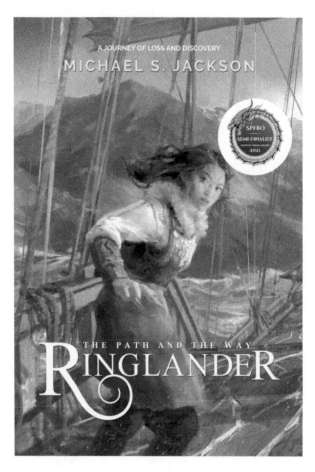

A JOURNEY OF LOSS AND DISCOVERY

MICHAEL S. JACKSON

SPFBO
SEMI-FINALIST
2021

THE PATH AND THE WAY

RINGLANDER

★★★★★

A wonderfully detailed and exceptionally well-done
fantasy story that stands out as one of the best titles I have
read this year. *Beth Tabler - Before We Go Blog*

AVAILABLE NOW FROM

Waterstones   BARNES&NOBLE

Lightning Source UK Ltd.
Milton Keynes UK
UKHW010728240622
404881UK00002B/107